Her Christmas Movie Kiss

Grace J. Croy

Cover Design by Blue Water Books

To Mom and Dad,
Who read all of my books, multiple times, and offer invaluable feedback.
My books are better because of you both.
Love you!

Chapter One

MEG

CHRISTMAS IS EVERYWHERE.

I feel it in the freezing Utah temperatures. Smell it in the scent of an incoming snowstorm. See it in the colored lights I pass in downtown Salt Lake City as I look for a place to park.

On a Friday night, five days before Christmas, there are hordes of shoppers, and finding street parking is impossible. Not that I allow the impossibility to flatten my happiness. Even the bustling crowds feel like Christmas.

And I *love* Christmas.

After twenty minutes of looking, I snag a space seconds after it's vacated. It's a few blocks away from the restaurant where I'm meeting my family, but the cold has never bothered me. I grab coins from my purse to put in the meter, only to find the last person left me an hour of free parking. Bonus. This is why December is awesome. People are kinder and more generous than at any other time of the year.

I tighten my scarf and stroll down the crowded street, a skip in my step. It's been eight months since I last visited my parents and twin brother, Matt, in Idaho Falls. I've missed them. Having my family here for Christmas is a special treat. My parents don't come down to Salt Lake often. Matt has never visited me, not once since I started the nursing program at the University of Utah nine years ago.

Until now.

I'm still in shock that they're here. I only found out a few hours ago when Mom called. She wanted to surprise me by booking a condo up the mountain at Nordquest Ski Resort for the next week. I'm only able to stay with them for a few days because, for the fourth year in a row, I work on Christmas Day. Usually, I don't mind working Christmas but this year with my family visiting, I am disappointed. A fact I won't focus on. I have three days in between to celebrate with my family and I'm excited about every one of them.

What delights me the most is the absence of Noah, Matt's best friend. Mom didn't mention him during our phone call, which is miraculous. Everywhere Matt goes, Noah follows, but not this year. I'll have three days to get to know my twin brother again. We should be close, closer than most siblings, since we spent so much time together in the womb. But that was a long time ago, and it makes me sad we're practically strangers these days. Matt is so busy with his successful career as a car salesman and his full social calendar, he can't find time for me.

When we were kids, we did everything together. We were best friends. Then middle school started, and with me more interested in choir and him in sports, we began to grow apart.

It was sophomore year of high school, when Noah and Matt both made the Varsity baseball team, that he pulled away completely. Matt and Noah became best friends, and I got left out. I felt invisible.

This week is my chance to get close to Matt again, like we were as kids. He won't have work or any of his friends to distract him. We'll have the chance to talk, play board games, and ski.

Without Noah.

This is what I've wanted for years, and I'm finally getting it this Christmas.

A bout of nervousness hits me. What if instead of drawing closer, he slips further away? Maybe I'll bore him.

My steps slow. People jostle me from all sides, the boulder in the middle of a fast-moving river. I step to the side and lean against a building.

Growing up, I was the bookish, quiet sister who lived in his shadow, while he was the outgoing, life-of-the-party older brother (by fifteen minutes). When I'm with my family, I slip back into the person I was in high school. Even now, as an adult, it's hard to fit into his busy, loud lifestyle.

Am I being ridiculous? Yes. That doesn't stop the worry from running rampant through my head.

An icy wind whips past, and I shiver. Someone's scarf blows across the sidewalk, and I watch it twirl up in the air. Just then, the clouds part and I catch sight of a single star in the sky.

I wish I may, I wish I might, have the wish I wish tonight: I wish to become close with Matt again, like we were as kids.

The clouds swarm, covering the patch of space. I take a breath and push the air down to my toes.

I'm being a chicken. My family is five minutes away, not three hours, and I'm wasting time holding up a wall. They came here to spend Christmas with me. The least I can do is meet them at the restaurant sooner rather than later.

A break comes in the pedestrian traffic from both directions, and I race across the sidewalk. At this moment, jaywalking sounds like a brilliant idea.

Why did the chicken cross the road? To prove to herself she wasn't afraid.

I step into the street between two parked cars, but instead of my foot hitting the road, it falls an extra eight inches into a pothole filled with freezing wet slush. I almost face-plant on the asphalt, but catch myself. The slush steals my shoe when I yank my foot out. I try to balance on one foot, but I do not possess the grace of a flamingo.

Slip, stumble, slip. My arms flail. Each slide brings me closer to speeding traffic. I'm pretty sure my head is about to crack like an egg if a car doesn't hit me first.

I close my eyes and prepare for the worst, when someone grabs the back of my coat, yanks me upright, and drags me back a few steps. I'm standing, balanced, and other than a freezing foot, in one piece.

"Are you okay?" the husky, deep voice behind me asks.

He's breathing just as fast as I am, his exhales warming my ear. I shiver, whether from the cold or his breath on my neck, I can't be sure.

Am I okay? My heart is banging around in my chest like a ping-pong ball, and I'm having a hard time focusing on anything beyond the firm hold the man has on my upper arms. He saved me from becoming a headline in the newspaper. Proof that strangers are kinder at Christmas.

Come January, I would have ended up as scrambled brains beneath a car's tire.

I glance to my left where the stranger holds tight to my biceps. He wears no gloves. From the glow of the street light shining above us, his fingers look strong, his nails trimmed. There's no gold band on his ring finger. His voice sounds not too old, not too young, but just right. I tally up his other assets. Amazing cologne, taller than me, expensive wool coat, and he saved my life. I've gone on dates with less to go on.

This could be my Christmas meet cute. In all the movies, the male and female leads meet in some surprising, embarrassing way. My current situation would definitely qualify.

"Yeah, I'm okay," I answer. My voice sounds breathy and quivers. Not the impression I'm going for, but I'm missing a shoe, and I almost died. I've lost my opportunity to give a good first impression, and possibly a second. I'll have to rely on my third.

I take a step out of his arms and turn. He's a good eight inches taller than I am, and as I look up, the street light creates a halo behind his head. It's impossible to make out his features, but his hair is short, his face is lean, and he has nice ears. I like what I can see.

"Thanks again," I say. "I'm Meg."

"Yeah, I know."

There's laughter and a touch of confusion in his voice. I can't imagine why, until I shuffle to the right to lean against a car and get my wet foot off the frozen asphalt. No longer blinded by the light, I recognize my rescuer. All words and any gratitude I felt moments before dries up.

Noah Murphy. My twin brother's best friend and the only person on this earth that I hate.

He's here.

I stood in his arms. I allowed his breath to caress my cheek. I actually believed this could be a romantic beginning to a long and wonderful relationship. My brain revolts, as does my stomach.

"You?" The word is torn from my throat, and I stumble away, back toward oncoming traffic.

He grabs the front of my coat and pulls me in his direction. I slap his hand away, but stay where I stand.

"Where did you come from?" I ask.

"The airport."

"What are you doing here?" I'm one hundred percent sure I know the answer, but I ask anyway hoping for a different one.

Noah's expression goes from worried to guarded. "I'm here for dinner."

"Not with my family, you're not."

He shakes his head as he squints in confusion. "I haven't seen you in over four years. What have I done this time to make you dislike me?"

"My memory is long."

He snorts a laugh. "We're not teenagers anymore. Can we call a truce?"

What does our age have to do with him showing up at Christmas and stealing my family's attention so there isn't any left for me? Maybe it shouldn't bother me now that I'm an adult of twenty-seven, but it does.

"I don't know," I say, bitterness tinging my words. "Can you act like a decent human for once in your life?"

"I did just save you from oncoming traffic. Is that decent enough?" His words are barely audible over the wind. He bends down and drags my shoe from the slush pit and drops it on the sidewalk. "See you inside."

See you inside. He can't threaten me like that and expect to get away with it.

But later. Right now, I have to catch up, and he's got a monster stride.

Chapter Two

MEG

I FOLLOW NOAH FOR A FEW BLOCKS, STAYING CLOSE, BUT NOT that close. He wheels a suitcase behind him, which only means bad news. I want to believe he's only here for dinner, but I can't ignore the evidence suggesting otherwise.

In the years since I last saw him, his appearance hasn't changed. He's still tall and broad-shouldered, with long legs and a nice butt.

Yeah, I don't like him, but I have an appreciation for art.

When he enters the restaurant, I'm just behind him. I quickly scan the tables until I find my parents sitting in a booth along the north wall. I push past, leaving him at the entrance, so I can get to my parents first. Once they see Noah, I'll be background noise. My parents love him like a favorite second son.

Mom notices my approach and stands to pull me into a hug. I lean in and soak up the love.

"How is my dear, sweet Meg?" she asks.

"So happy to see you."

I miss my family. I've thought about moving closer to them, but it's easier to ignore that I'm their least favorite child, third even to the interloper, when I live two hundred miles away.

I don't blame them for loving me least. They're outgoing, throw a lot of dinner parties, and live to be social like Matt. Growing up, it caused misunderstandings and arguments. They even sent me to therapy because they were sure it was depression that made me prefer nights at home and a small social circle. Things got better between us as I grew older. They appreciate who I am, but they just don't get me. When I turned eighteen, I moved to Utah where I could be authentically me without having to validate my existence.

Since then, we've all settled into reality. We're different, but we love each other. They just love Matt (and Noah) more.

Dad takes his turn for a hug. He isn't much taller than I am. My whole family is on the shorter side, with Matt being the tallest at five feet nine inches, and Mom the shortest at five feet three inches. Noah is over six feet tall, which makes it obvious he doesn't belong. *One of these things is not like the others.* I'm the only one who notices.

"Where's Matt?" I ask. I need to give him a hug before he sees Noah.

"He ran to the bathroom," Mom says. She widens her eyes and leans close to whisper, "He has an upset stomach."

The way she acts like this is a secret probably means he's been visiting the bathroom a lot. I hope he feels better by tomorrow. This is Christmas! No one should be sick over the Christmas holiday.

I take a step toward the bathrooms to wait outside for Matt—yes, I'm that desperate for a few minutes with him alone—when I hear his voice over the rumble of restaurant chatter. He and Noah are heading in our direction. I'm too late.

Matt is unquestionably handsome. His dark hair is a rumpled mess, though I'm sure it took him twenty minutes to style. His sharp cheekbones, bronze complexion, and deep brown eyes meant all the girls in high school were in love with him. He knew it, too.

Even though we're twins, we look nothing alike. My hair isn't dark like his, but it's not blond either. It's that in-between non-color some might call dishwater. I'm short and curvy and have yet to grow out of my squishy, plump cheeks. I have an aunt who still pinches them every time she sees me.

My parents greet Noah with hugs and exclamations.

My brother squeezes me tight for one second before my release.

"How's it going?" he asks, as he rubs the top of my head like I'm a troll doll and he's rubbing me for good luck. "Staying out of trouble?"

It's annoying when he treats me like I'm fifteen years younger and not fifteen minutes.

He slides onto the bench without waiting for an answer. Noah follows, ignoring my existence as he takes *my* seat. Rude. I'm forced to take the chair placed at the end of the booth. Noah's suitcase cuts into my legroom. Also, rude.

"Mom said your roommates were coming?" Matt says as he looks over the menu.

I'm not surprised he failed to read the text I sent an hour

ago when my roommates turned down the invitation to dinner. He's not great at reading texts. Sometimes it takes days for him to respond to me. Tonight, I'm sure he's only concerned about their absence because they're female, and he loves female attention.

"They had other plans," I say.

I wish my two roommates were here. I'd feel a lot better if I had my best friends with me since Matt has Noah. Unfortunately, Layla's on a date with her loser ex-boyfriend, and Livy wanted to stay in and watch a movie.

I take my designated role as the silent observer as conversation volleys between the other four. It's all about Noah and his work travels as a consultant. He goes around the country, saving businesses from financial collapse. My parents haven't seen him since October and they want all the news. No matter that none of them have seen me since April. I talk to my parents on the phone at least once a week, but they talk to Noah just as often.

People pass behind and knock into me on their way to the bathroom. Each time a server comes by with a full tray, I scoot a little closer to the table and hope they don't trip on a chair leg. The edge of the table digs into my ribs, but that's an easier pain to focus on than the one poking my heart.

When there's a slight break in the conversation, I ask, "How long are you staying, Noah?"

I cross my fingers under the table, hoping he's only here for tonight, and I'll have the Christmas I wished for earlier. His suitcase might mean he's traveling on, and this is just a layover.

Noah doesn't look up from buttering his roll.

"I'm staying at Nordquest for the week, then traveling

back to Idaho Falls with your family where I'll stay until after the new year."

"Didn't I tell you?" Mom says.

No. She did not.

I slouch in my chair, my hope dashed. I won't have Matt to myself, not for a single second. Tonight is a preview of the rest of my week. My stupid wish on a star. It was probably a planet. The light pollution in this city is terrible. Just my luck, it violates wishing rules to make a wish on a planet. Now, I'm getting cursed.

"When are you coming up, Meg?" Dad asks.

"Tomorrow night after my shift," I answer. "I'll get there around seven, depending on the weather."

I will beg my roommates to spend the next few days with me and my family at Nordquest. I can't spend the week as the odd one out again. I can't.

"We plan to go skiing tomorrow while you work," Mom says. "We know you don't like skiing."

That's not true, it's just that every time we've gone skiing as a family, Noah tags along, and I end up skiing alone. That's why I return to the lodge early, not because I dislike it.

Before I can explain, Noah turns his attention to me for the first time since we sat down. I forgot how intense his gaze can be. I freeze like a rabbit in the headlights of an oncoming diesel truck.

"Matt says you have to work on Christmas?" he asks.

"Yep," I say. "I have work early, so I'll leave Nordquest Tuesday night, on Christmas Eve."

"We'll have Christmas dinner on Christmas Eve," Mom explains. "Then open gifts before she has to go."

Dad chimes in next. "There's a party at the lodge that

night. We bought tickets, so after Meg leaves, we'll go mingle."

"Christmas day," Matt says, "We ski."

Did they come to Utah to visit me? Because it sounds like they can't wait until I'm gone.

"I would like to go skiing at least one day," I say, but the conversation has already moved on to picking out a Christmas tree after we finish dinner. It's like I haven't spoken at all.

"We'll decorate the tree on Sunday when Meg can be with us," Mom says. "I brought lights and ornaments, but we can also string popcorn into a garland and make gingerbread men ornaments."

"That sounds fun," I say.

I inherited my love of Christmas from Mom. She's the best at making the holidays special and is an event planner by profession. I might not have enjoyed the epic parties she threw at our house when I was a kid, but I loved the special touches she incorporated into our holidays.

Matt doesn't appreciate special holiday touches like I do. He rolls his eyes. "Noah and I can take another ski day."

Of course, he would say that.

"No," I begin, "This is a family Christmas. We should spend the day together."

"Dad," Matt says, speaking over me, "You should join us. We're at a ski resort; we should ski."

Dad nods, pondering. "Maybe I will."

Mom shakes her head, but indulgently. Looks like it will be just the women decorating while the men go play.

Throughout our meal, I try a few more times to interject my opinions or thoughts into the conversation, but any words I manage to get out are stomped on before I finish. It's a normal interaction with my family. My parents and Matt are verbose, loud, and opinionated. The only unusual thing about the evening is Matt hardly touches his steak and potatoes. He's always had a sensitive stomach. Poor guy. I feel bad for him.

After dinner, we walk a few blocks to a tree lot. Mom and Dad follow behind and look at the store window Christmas displays.

Noah and Matt lead the way, laughing and talking. Neither of them draw me into the conversation.

I'm left to walk alone. We may be adults, but not much has changed since high school. All my hopes for an opportunity to spend time with my brother are dead.

Matt is my twin. He should be my best friend. But Noah put a wedge between us years ago, and I'm not sure how to dislodge him.

Chapter Three

MEG

When I arrive back at my apartment, all I want to do is vent to my roommates. Sadly, my apartment is dark. Livy's probably asleep. Today was her last day teaching middle school English before the holiday break, and she was worn out when I left earlier. Layla's bedroom door is open, her room empty. I'll wait for her to get home. I need to talk to someone about how Noah has torpedoed my holiday.

I turn the TV to a Christmas movie and collapse on the couch. Christmas movies might be the one thing to get me through my disappointment. There's just something about watching two people overcoming the odds to fall in love while singing carols and decorating trees that lightens my heart.

Just as the ending credits roll on another perfect, happy ending, a key sounds in the front door lock.

"You're up," Layla says as she enters. She glances at the wall clock. It's midnight. "I expected you to be asleep."

"I wanted to wait for you." I'm not selfish, so instead of jumping into the injustices in my life, I begin with, "How is Spencer? Did you have a nice dinner?"

I'm not a fan of Spencer, so I hope the answer is no and that they aren't getting back together for the fourth time this year.

She sighs. I'm sure it's supposed to sound happy, but it comes across as exhausted. "He proposed."

I sit up and lean forward. "And you said no?"

She giggles. "I said yes."

My lips flap open a few times, but I have no words. I'm sure Spencer is a good guy, but he isn't good to Layla. He's too busy with work and always puts her on the back burner. She's unhappy when they're dating, which is why they keep breaking up. I can't understand why she would say yes to *marriage*.

She holds out her hand and steps closer. "It's a beautiful ring, don't you think?"

It's huge. I'm amazed she can lift her hand. On a sunny day, she'll blind everyone within a mile radius.

"Wow."

"Yeah." She cradles her hand to her chest and sits on the couch next to me. "We're flying to Maine tomorrow morning to meet his family and surprise them with the engagement."

I can't keep up. "Isn't this a little sudden? You haven't seen him in months—"

"Just seven weeks."

Like that's so much better. "Suddenly he shows up, takes

you to dinner, proposes *marriage*, and you're set to go meet his family *tomorrow morning*?"

"Yeah, it's like a fairy tale, don't you think?"

Closer to a nightmare. She doesn't sound happy, definitely doesn't look happy, and she isn't the type to make rash decisions.

"What's wrong, Layla? Why are you doing this?"

She won't meet my gaze. "Because I love Spencer."

"No. You don't." I can say that with one hundred percent confidence.

She stands and hurries to the hallway. "I do. Have a Merry Christmas."

Her bedroom door closes. Something is up, but I can't hog-tie her to a chair until she comes to her senses.

She's too smart to fall for Spencer's proposal, at least for longer than a few days. She's going to figure things out and break up with him for good. I wish I could help her come to this realization, but it's something she'll have to figure out for herself.

I collapse onto the couch as I come to my own realization. Layla can't come with me to Nordquest for the week.

I still have Livy. Her other option is to stay here alone. She may be more introverted than I am, but she won't want to be alone over her Christmas break.

THE NEXT MORNING, HEAVY CLOUDS HANG OVER THE VALLEY. I check the weather report, and a huge storm will hit later this afternoon. It may keep me and Livy from making it up the mountain tonight. That wouldn't be so bad.

I get to the hospital by six for our shift debriefing and receive my assignments for the day. We're short-staffed because of illness, so I have six patients instead of my regular four. I'm not upset, because I'm working with Doctor Doug, my long-time crush. Telesa winks at me from across the room. She knows how I feel about him and is nothing but encouraging.

When our meeting ends, we leave together.

"Let me know how it goes with The Doctor," she says softly.

"Will do."

It proves to be a busy day, which is great because while visiting patients, I have very little brain space to stew about Matt and Noah's bromance. I don't take breaks because when I sit, my eyelids become too heavy to fight off drowsiness.

Midmorning, I get a text from Livy.

Livy: *Did you hear Layla's news?*

No matter how miserable I'm going to be stuck with Noah for the week, I bet Layla will be even more miserable with Spencer.

Meg: *CAN YOU BELIEVE IT? I'm hoping it won't last past Jan first.*

Livy: *I'm optimistic. December 24.*

I type out a text asking if she's up for a few days with my family, but before I hit send, her next message comes through.

Livy: *Since you both have plans, I'm heading up to Eden's place today.*

She's going to Wyoming to stay with her sister?

I collapse in a chair. My good mood deflates. Mom has Dad. Matt has Noah. I have no one.

Meg: *I'll miss you, but I understand. Be careful! The snowstorm is supposed to be epic!*

There's nothing to do but continue my rounds. When I enter Mr. Murdock's room, Doctor Doug is already inside. He glances over and his flawless smile grows. He should be a model for teeth-whitening commercials. His lips are never chapped like mine are during the winter, and his teeth are perfectly straight. I wouldn't call them dimples, but his cheeks crease perfectly when he smiles.

I also like the adorable cowlick on the crown of his head. And his round Harry Potter glasses. And the perfectly pressed slacks he wears at the hospital.

"You're in excellent hands with Meg," he says to Mr. Murdock. He winks at me. "She's my favorite nurse."

Another tally in his favor is he knows my name. That shouldn't impress me, but it does because most doctors don't know me as anything other than "Nurse," even after years of working with them.

I'm half in love with Doug, and though I think he likes me too, he only flirts. I keep hoping for a date, even a meal together in the break room, but nada.

My desperation for his attention outside of work just shows how pathetic my social life has become in the past year since I broke up with my last boyfriend.

Doctor Doug draws closer. His hand lands on my shoulder. His mouth is only inches away from my ear as he leans in. Is this it? Is he about to ask if we can grab a coffee in the cafeteria together?

"Let me know if Mr. Murdock needs anything."

He gives me one more gut-punch smile before disappearing out the door.

Maybe next time.

I shake off my disappointment and chart Mr. Murdock's stats.

As I check on patients throughout the morning, I notice the clouds outside grow thicker. The promised storm is definitely coming in and sooner than predicted. By lunch, snow is falling.

I text Livy to see how she's doing on her drive to her sister's place, but don't get a response. With the howl of the wind outside, I worry. I check the weather in Wyoming where she's headed and see the storm has moved in that direction. I bite my nails as I watch the snowfall outside and hope she's okay.

Layla texts to let me know she's landed in Maine. I text back, asking for details.

Layla: *I'm okay. Don't worry about me. I'll see you next week.*

Well then. It doesn't sound like she plans to give us regular updates.

Back to work.

Twelve hours after my arrival, it's time for me to head out. I'm gathering my stuff from my locker when I receive a text from an unknown number.

Unknown: *Hey Meg, this is Livy. My phone got wet so if you've been texting me, that's why I haven't responded. I borrowed a phone, so don't text me back because I probably won't be able to respond. I'm okay. All is well.*

What!? Why didn't she borrow her sister's phone? Did she even get to her sister's house? I call, hoping to catch her before she gives the phone back to whomever she borrowed it from.

She answers. "Hello?"

"Why is your phone wet? Did you get to your sister's okay?"

I move to the window and look out into the snowy night.

"No," she says. "I'm at an Inn about an hour-and-a-half away from Eden's. My car slid into a river."

This is awful. It seems Christmas plans aren't working out for anyone in our apartment.

"Are you hurt?" I ask.

"No, I'm fine." She sounds sad and tired, but that's nothing compared to what might have been. "My car is probably totaled. Some guy came by and rescued me. He let me borrow his phone to call you."

I'm relieved to know she's somewhere warm and safe. I know what can happen to someone who gets wet in the middle of a snowstorm.

"You're sure you're okay?" I ask. "Do you need me to come rescue you?"

She laughs wearily. "I'm okay. Promise. I don't want anyone driving on those roads."

Since she's fine physically, what she needs now is some cheering up. I collapse into a chair and say thoughtfully, "Is he married?"

Her voice turns serious. "Did you catch the part where I slid off the road, down an incline, and into a river?"

We're not dwelling on that, or I won't be able to sleep tonight.

"I caught the part about a cute guy rescuing you," I say. "He is cute, right?"

"It doesn't matter."

"That must be a yes. And if he were married, then you would've just told me, so he must be single."

She sighs dramatically, and I know she's going to play along. I've worn her down.

"Yeah, okay," she says. "He's cute, and I don't think he has a wife, but he has a daughter and a girlfriend."

I ignore everything except his cuteness and skip to the good part. "Livy! You're in a Hallmark movie!"

She laughs. "Really? That's what you're taking away from my near-death experience?"

Her voice is lighter. My plan is working. I'm just glad it was only *near* death.

"You said yourself you're fine. Always so dramatic."

She snorts. "I'm dramatic?"

I quickly think through the two dozen Christmas movies I've watched over the last month and land on the one that most resembles Livy's current situation.

"Remember the movie last week where the city girl goes to the country to visit her grandpa, but on the way a storm hits, and she crashes into the hot doctor's truck? She's stranded with him for the holidays, and they fall in love!"

I laugh, delighted that I've found the perfect movie to fit her predicament.

"Jay isn't a doctor," she says, back to her serious voice. "Nor did I crash into him. And hello! He has a girlfriend."

"Pshaw. In every Hallmark movie, the girlfriend is not the right fit for the hero of the story. Forget about her."

She sighs, but it isn't as weighted and sad as when we first started talking. "What have you heard from Layla? How's it going with Spencer's family?"

I let her derail my fun for Layla. "She sent a text to our group chat when she arrived in Maine, but it seems she doesn't plan to keep us updated on developments."

"Maybe she's realized her mistake and isn't ready to admit it yet?"

"Fingers crossed."

"I'm sure she's okay."

"If something is seriously wrong, she'll let us know," I say.

A coworker peeks into the break room. "There's a question about a patient. The doctor wants to see you in room 175 before you leave."

I nod to let her know I heard then say into the phone, "Hey, I gotta go. Keep me updated on your romance?"

Livy snorts again. "I'm leaving tomorrow. There won't be much to update you on."

She isn't the only one who could use a distraction from life right now so I hope her evening is eventful.

"We'll see."

Chapter Four

MEG

THINGS ARE NOT GOING MY WAY.

By the time I leave the hospital, the storm has stopped.

The plows have done their job and cleared most of the roads.

My suitcase waits in the back of my car.

I have no excuse not to head up the mountain tonight.

I do hard things. Like being civil to Noah. *I do distasteful things*. Like spending Christmas with Noah. *I can overcome great disappointment.* Like being overlooked by my family because of Noah.

It's normally a thirty-minute drive to Nordquest, but traffic moves slowly and the snow is deeper the higher I travel up the mountain, so it takes over an hour. Even with the Christmas music blaring, it gives me a long time to be alone with my thoughts. Unfortunately, most of those thoughts circle around Noah.

I have eleven years of anger built up toward him, but at the center of it all is the pain of losing him as my best friend before he was ever my brother's friend.

The first time I saw Noah was in second-period English class during our freshman year of high school. He was a new student starting out in a new school in mid-February, the dreariest month of the year. For an entire week, he looked out the window and never once opened *Romeo and Juliet.*

I loved Winnie-the-Pooh when I was a little kid, and he reminded me of Eeyore. I could see the black rain cloud over his head, drenching him in sadness.

I've never liked seeing sorrow etched so deeply into someone's eyes, and I decided I would be a Tigger in his life. I invited him to sit with my friends at lunch, and so, over the next few weeks, our friendship was forged.

Soon, we were no longer Eeyore and Tigger, but Winnie and Piglet. Best friends. Inseparable.

He came over to my house every day after school because he hated his empty house. His parents had just divorced, and his dad worked sixty-hour weeks at his failing business.

Noah and I did homework together or watched movies. Mostly we talked. I'd never felt so comfortable around someone before, definitely not a guy.

During the summer, we played baseball in the park. I would play catcher to his pitcher, or lob him the ball, and he'd hit it further than I wanted to run to find it.

It devastated him that he missed tryouts for the Junior Varsity team the January before. His plans involved getting a baseball scholarship and then playing in the major leagues. He felt the pressure to show college scouts what he could do.

Over that year, the growing distance between Matt and me didn't sting so much because I had Noah. I expected us to be best friends forever.

Then baseball tryouts came around in January of the following year.

On the day of tryouts, Noah and I met at my locker after school. His hands shook, and he couldn't keep still. He paced three steps in each direction. The weight of his future hung on what happened over the next few days.

I caught his arm, pulled him down close to me, went up on my tiptoes, and kissed him. I don't know why I did it, except I wanted to, and I thought it might distract him. It was supposed to be a short good luck kiss, but he kissed me back. Like, really kissed me back. It was my first kiss and a riot of butterflies erupted in my stomach.

He pulled back and asked, "Will you go to Winter Formal with me?"

It was four weeks away, and I had hoped he would ask. "Yes."

He kissed me again, this time quickly, then went off toward the gym. Before disappearing inside, he turned and waved.

Tryouts went better than anyone could guess, and not only did he make the Varsity team as a sophomore, but so did Matt. Overnight, Noah skyrocketed to a level of popularity where I wasn't welcome.

He never ate lunch with me again. He stopped walking with me between classes. He didn't meet me at my locker after school anymore.

He left me behind.

The truth hit me hard. When he didn't have anyone else,

I was a nice placeholder. Once he had other friends, I was no longer needed.

Matt's the one who told me Noah asked Vanessa Harding to Winter Formal. He was really nice about it and broke the news with a pint of ice cream and a box of my favorite cereal.

"Sorry, Meg, but Noah has a reputation to protect now. He can't go to the dance with you. You're not popular, you know? He wanted me to tell you he's sorry."

I cried for a week and then went to the dance stag with a couple of my "unpopular" friends.

All of this was heartbreaking, yes, but something I would have recovered from eventually if we'd grown apart and stuck with our different social circles.

But that wasn't what happened.

The Monday after Winter Formal, I came home from school and Noah was in my living room. I thought he was there for me. I'd waited for him to remember our friendship, the promise of that kiss. The thrill of seeing him lasted maybe two seconds until I realized the truth. He hadn't come to see me. He was there with Matt.

Noah traded up to the better twin. I lost my brother and my best friend in just a few weeks.

Once baseball season began, my parents went to every game and Noah was folded into our family in a way he wasn't when he was my friend. He was at my house all the time just like before, but everything was different.

When he was there, I left or went into my room. Matt told me I made him uncomfortable with my staring. I didn't think I stared, but I made sure I never looked in his general direction in case Noah thought I was looking at him.

Noah never spoke to me, even when we were at the same

dinner table every night. I wanted to believe it was because of guilt, but if he felt guilty about dropping me as a friend, stealing my family, or taking someone else to Winter Formal, then why didn't he ever apologize?

If only I could have left all of that in high school, but Noah is still around. He and Matt went to the same university. They go on vacations together with the same group of friends every year. He visits my parents more than I do. He comes to every major family holiday, which is why I don't anymore.

How could I have ever believed he would miss out on Christmas this year? I'm stupidly optimistic.

By the time I reach Nordquest, I'm in a foul mood.

Nordquest is a small, mountain community nestled in a narrow valley. The main road through town is essentially a one-mile loop. Small shops, restaurants, a bakery, rental homes, and even a lake that freezes over in the winter make up the small town.

As I drive the loop toward the ski resort, I pass shops with brightly lit holiday window displays and happy people walking down the street. My roommates and I come up for a day at the beginning of every December to look in the shops and enjoy the hot chocolate. This town is everything Christmas should be.

The ski lodge is set back from the road, a luxury resort ten stories high. Each condo has its own balcony, and light from the many rooms shines out onto the parking lot. I wonder if my family has noticed I'm late. They're probably relaxing after a fun day of skiing and haven't spared a thought for me. At least, they haven't called or texted to see if I'm on my way.

I grab my suitcase and head inside.

The lobby is impressive. The ceiling goes up to the third story, and a grand staircase splits the space in half. To the left is a Christmas tree, two stories high, lit with so many small lights it glows. If it were outside, the astronauts on the space station could use it as a landmark for Utah. A fireplace is along one wall, a fire blazing, with guests scattered on comfy couches. Carols play over the sound system.

The atmosphere is festive, bright, and happy. Staff smile at me as I pass the front desk to the elevator. A small child skips past me and waves.

Christmas is literally the best season.

All the angst I've carried since Noah showed up last night dissipates. Yeah, it sucks that he'll be here with my family all week, but even he can't ruin Christmas.

I take the elevator up to the sixth floor, look for the room number Mom gave me last night, and knock. I can't contain my smile.

My charitable mood is put to the test immediately when Noah opens the door, a dour expression in place.

"Merry Christmas," I sing out.

"What's so merry about it?" he asks. His eyebrows are low like the storm clouds outside. He may as well be saying, "Bah humbug."

"It's Christmas," I reiterate as I move past him into the condo. I choose to ignore his bad attitude, right along with his very existence. "Everything is merry at Christmas."

The condo is larger than I expected. There's a great room with a living area and an updated kitchen. It even has a double oven, which Mom and I will utilize for Christmas Eve dinner. The tree my brother picked out last night is in the corner, lit with colored lights, but otherwise undecorated.

There's the bathroom and a hallway that leads to the promised three bedrooms.

I remove my coat and leave my suitcase by the table, then head directly to the refrigerator. I'm starving, and I'm sure there are dinner leftovers to be had.

"Did you get my texts?" Noah asks from the other side of the kitchen island.

"Why would I want texts from you?"

I'm distracted by the lack of a waiting meal. The fridge is stuffed with food for the week, but I don't see any dinner leftovers. Maybe they went out to eat? But then where is my takeout box? Mom wouldn't forget to pick something up for me.

I take another look around the condo. It's so quiet. Where are my parents? Where's Matt? Matt and Noah are like flashing lights and a migraine. Where one is, the other follows behind.

Noah stands with his arms crossed over his chest and a scowl slashed across his beautiful face. I really do loathe the man. Especially his broad shoulders. And thick dark hair. And brown, hypnotizing eyes. Ugh, no one has a right to look that handsome. If life were fair, he'd be ugly on the outside to match the ugliness on the inside.

"I've been texting you all day," he says.

"I didn't get any texts." I turn to the cupboards to see what snacks mom brought.

"Maybe I got your number wrong?"

Or maybe I blocked his number years ago. One or the other. "Where's my family?"

"That's what I was texting you about. They're sick."

I stop rummaging through the cupboards and look over my shoulder. "What?"

"I think it's the stomach flu."

Well, that might ruin Christmas.

Chapter Five

NOAH

MEG'S CONFUSION MORPHS INTO A SCOWL. SHE GLARES AS IF it's my fault her family is sick.

"The flu?" she says like it's a word she's never heard before. "How did that happen?"

I'm exhausted by her hatred. I haven't seen her for years and yet she glares at me as if I am the source of all of her troubles.

"Usually by the transfer of a virus from one host to another," I say dryly. "But you're the nurse. You tell me."

Her eyes narrow as she closes the cupboard and storms past me and down the hallway. I follow behind at a much calmer pace. When I catch up, she's inside Matt's room, sitting on the edge of the bed, feeling his forehead with the back of her hand.

"How do you feel?" she murmurs.

"Awful," Matt says, his voice weak. He didn't sound that

bad when I brought him water an hour ago. He's either gone downhill fast, or he's begging for sympathy.

"Sore throat? Body aches? Chills?" Meg asks.

"A little. Mostly stomach cramps. A headache."

"Diarrhea? Vomiting?"

Matt groans. He's definitely looking for sympathy. "Yeah. All of that."

"You don't have a fever." Her voice is calm. The stress and worry I've felt all day melts away, and she isn't even talking to me. This kindness is a side of her I haven't seen in a long time. "Have you been around anyone sick in the last few days?"

"Not that I know of."

"What did you eat yesterday?"

Matt details everything he ate and Meg listens patiently. She's an incredible nurse. If I were sick, she's who I would want taking care of me.

Meg pats Matt's hand tenderly before leaving his bedside. Once in the hallway, she stomps past me once again and heads to the master bedroom at the end of the hall. This time I don't follow. It's awkward talking with Matt's parents while they're sick in bed. In their pajamas.

I head to the kitchen and fill a pot with water before putting it on the stove. If I had to guess from Meg's earlier rummaging, she's hungry. I dump a jar of sauce in a pan and heat it up while I wait for the water to boil.

"What have you done for them?" Meg asks as she steps into the kitchen.

"I've kept them hydrated and given them Tylenol. Like Google told me to do for the flu."

She begrudgingly shrugs. "I guess that's good, but I don't

think it's the flu. My guess is the tacos they had for lunch yesterday. That's good news for us since they're not contagious, but they'll probably feel ill for another day or two."

"I texted you multiple times to let you know they were sick."

She won't meet my gaze, but finds her fingernails fascinating.

I study her as she ignores me. Her green scrubs (decorated with mini Santa hats, stockings, reindeer, and mistletoe), bring out the green flecks in her eyes. It's pathetic that after all these years and her obvious dislike, she's still the girl I've never gotten over.

The last time I saw her was her parents' Fourth of July party four-and-a-half years ago. She barely looked at me then, too, but of course, she wouldn't because her boyfriend came with her. I still remember the bite of jealousy I felt each time he looped his arm over her shoulders or whispered in her ear.

"You didn't get my texts, did you?" I ask.

I told her family I'd take care of contacting her, and I tried. Her number hasn't changed since high school, so if she didn't get my messages, that means she blocked my number.

I don't understand how she can still resent me. I messed up, but that was a long time ago. Matt has told me innumerable times that Meg doesn't forgive easily, but eleven years?

She grabs her coat from the back of a kitchen chair. "I should go to the convenience store and get some Pepto Bismol. It'll help calm their stomachs."

"I can go," I offer.

"No, I will. I need the air."

Is that code for *I need to get away from you?*

Before leaving, she stops by the stove and peers into the saucepan where the bottled spaghetti sauce is bubbling.

"Spaghetti?" she asks.

"Yeah. Is that okay?"

A shrug. "Sure." She's out the door.

I go out on the balcony and sit on one of the wire chairs. The winter air bites into my skin and my breath instantly fogs, but I don't grab my coat. The cold makes my wrist ache, but I don't grab my brace. A few minutes with Meg, and I feel I should punish myself for being an idiot sixteen-year-old kid.

I spot Meg below, walking across the snowy parking lot toward town.

When Matt called a few days ago to let me know about the change in plans for Christmas, I was hopeful about seeing Meg. I thought all her anger toward me would have burned out by now. Ha! She's determined to keep punishing me. I can't understand why.

It's strange to remember that Meg was my first friend in Idaho Falls. She became the bright spot in my life after moving to a new town following my parents' divorce. I lost all the friends I grew up with. My mom moved halfway across the country. Dad worked all the time.

But I had Meg. We did everything together. What I remember most is how much fun we had. She was friendly to everyone, but only a few people were lucky enough to see the silly, loud, sometimes obnoxious side of her. I was one of those lucky ones.

Then sophomore year baseball tryouts. Making the

varsity team was the best thing to happen to me, but also the worst. It set my course for the next seven years. But I lost Meg.

I knew Matt before tryouts. He was the star player of the Junior Varsity baseball team, but it wasn't until we both made the Varsity team that we became friends. He wasn't my only new friend. My social circle expanded overnight. I had never had so much attention from my peers, and it went to my head. For a few weeks, my popularity blinded me, and I lost my best friend.

I missed her, but by the time I tried to apologize, she'd moved on. She didn't like the spotlight I now stood in and didn't want to hang out with me anymore. Every time I went to Matt's after practice, she disappeared into her room. During dinner, she wouldn't look in my direction.

Matt told me to give her space. To not hassle her. Let her come to me. I've done as he suggested. For eleven years.

I still miss her. It makes no logical sense. We were friends for a year in high school, and we haven't been close for half our lives. Yet she's the girl I think about when I can't sleep. She's the one who got away.

Last night, as I walked to the restaurant, I saw her on the sidewalk, leaning against a building and looking wistfully up at the sky. I slowed down to stare at her. I couldn't look away. A feeling of rightness settled in my chest ... until she ran out into the street. I ran after her.

I can't forget how it felt to hold her in my arms, her back against my chest. For a few seconds, she didn't detest me. She smiled. At me. It was like the sun after weeks of rain or a home-cooked meal after eating fast food for a month.

Until she figured out *I* was her rescuer.

My disappointment and frustration with this Christmas situation has put me in a funk. Matt, Calvin, and Judy are sick. Meg still loathes me for a mistake I made eleven years ago. My parents are once again using me as the go-between in their fight for the last word. I thought their animosity would cool off after their divorce, but it's only gotten stronger. They don't know how to live without each other, or at least without their shared bitterness.

Everything would be okay if Meg at least tolerated me. Her hostility reminds me too much of the house I grew up in.

The kitchen timer beeps, and I head inside to drain the pasta.

Meg returns ten minutes later and walks past me into the hallway. I dish her some food and place her plate on the table next to mine.

I rub my sweaty hands down my pant legs. This is the first time we've been alone together since high school. I try to come up with a topic of conversation she might engage in, but when she returns, she grabs her plate and walks to the other end of the table ... and then to the couch where she grabs the TV remote.

I'm not prepared for my disappointment. I should've been. Did I really expect her to talk to me when she can't even look at me?

A carol blares from the TV. I'm at an angle to the television, but I can see the screen well enough to know there are a dozen carolers walking through a small town decorated with Christmas lights. A man has a tug-a-war with a dog over a scarf until he stumbles backward and falls into a snowdrift.

Meg's frown turns into a smile at the stupid scene. Within minutes, her eyebrows lift, her cheeks pink, and her eyes sparkle.

She's lovely.

Christmas has always looked good on her. She's a cheerful person by nature (unless I'm nearby), but in December, she glows with joy. I don't understand why it has this power over her. It's just one day out of three-hundred and sixty-five.

I don't dislike Christmas, but I don't love it either. Growing up, it meant more arguing between my parents, usually about money. Christmas morning, I felt guilty receiving gifts I knew they couldn't afford. I always got a ton because they wanted to prove to the other who was the better parent.

Until I met Meg, I hadn't understood what Christmas could mean. The family. The traditions. The lights. The laughter. She feels genuine joy throughout December.

I'm not sure the rest of her family feels the same. Matt's focus is on presents, given and received. Judy loves any reason to throw a party, but stresses about achieving perfection. Calvin picks up extra shifts at work to pay for everything, so he's not home much in the evenings.

Why all the hype and expense for one day? And why are so many movies dedicated to the holiday?

The sickly sweet happiness Meg's current movie is peddling makes me nauseous. Even compared to Meg's happy family, it's closer to a fairy tale than reality.

I pull out my laptop and log into my work email. It's empty. I have nothing to do. I travel all over the United States and help companies restructure, so they don't close their doors. My last account ended yesterday before I flew into Salt Lake City, and I'm not getting assigned a new one until January. I'm on a forced two-week vacation. Normally that would be great, but I'm stuck at the top of a mountain with a person who barely tolerates me.

I put the dirty dishes in the dishwasher. Stow the extra food in the fridge. Wipe down the counters. I even sweep the floor, though there isn't much to sweep up.

Finally, the movie ends and the credits roll. My relief is short-lived because, after a few previews for more Christmas movies, a new one starts. Does this channel play twenty-four hours of constant Christmas?

After an hour of listening to the inane conversation coming from the television while playing a game on my phone, I know I won't last to the end of a second movie. It's a similar plot. Even some of the actors are the same.

It's easy enough to walk over and steal the remote from the coffee table. I press the power button.

"Hey!" Meg looks up and holds out her hand. "Give the remote back. I like this one."

My eyes widen. "You've seen it before, and you still want to watch it?"

"It's a good one," she says.

"As opposed to a bad one? How can you tell the difference?"

Her eyes narrow. "What do you want?"

I want your forgiveness. I want to be your friend. I want a peaceful Christmas break.

I go with something attainable.

"I don't want to watch any more Christmas movies. They're terrible."

"They're festive."

"They lie."

"They spread Christmas cheer and love."

"They're completely unrealistic," I say. "The woman started the movie detesting the man and then they decorate a tree, and she suddenly likes him? Who comes up with this stuff?"

"Brilliant writers."

She's being purposefully obtuse.

I fold my arms and lean forward. "Do you actually believe it's realistic to go from hate to love in a matter of hours?"

"Does it matter if it's realistic? It's romantic."

I've always known Meg possessed a sentimental heart, but this is going too far. "I could write a better script, and it would actually make sense and be twice as romantic."

She rolls her eyes. "I'd like to see you try. Now, will you give me back the remote?"

I can't. The thought of watching these movies for the next few days while being simultaneously ignored is akin to having my fingernails ripped off. Maybe torture is Meg's plan for me this week. That doesn't mean I can't come up with a better one. Even this argument is preferable to being treated like I don't exist.

Maybe ... I can learn from this movie about enemies becoming friends. I've offered her so many apologies through the years for overlooking her in high school, but she's never accepted any of them. The next few days might be my chance to prove to her I've changed. I'm not that stupid kid anymore.

I point to the corner where the tree is waiting for

decorations. "How about instead of watching people do Christmas stuff, we actually do Christmas stuff? Like decorating the tree?"

"No."

She snatches the remote from my grip. Her touch is like a brand on my skin. I fist my hand and ignore the heat her fingers leave behind.

She turns on the TV in the middle of a drug commercial. As the voiceover describes all the possible negative side effects while happy people have a picnic in the park, I yell over the commercial, "Why not?"

She glares up at me again, her expression fierce, as she yells back, "Because I don't want to spend time with you."

"But what about the couple in the movie? They don't want to spend time together, but they do, and they start to like each other."

"I'm not going to suddenly like you just because we decorate a tree. Movies aren't real." She flings her hands up in the air like she's lost all patience. "They're a fantasy."

I know movies are fake. I was worried she didn't.

She turns up the volume.

I yell louder. "It's nice you know these stories aren't based in reality, but that doesn't mean we can't have a nice evening decorating a tree."

"Can you two shut up!"

We both turn to see Matt leaning against the wall, his face pale and his arms limp.

Meg mutes the TV. "Sorry. Did we wake you?"

"You probably woke the entire floor," he says. "Can you keep it down?"

"Yeah, sorry."

"We'll stop arguing," I promise.

Meg snorts.

Matt smirks. "Thanks." He disappears around the corner and a second later his door clicks shut.

The room is silent. It's nice after the awful movie.

"All I'm asking," I say, "Is that we turn off the TV and do something else."

"But I want to watch the movie."

"You said yourself that it isn't real. Let's do something real." I'm close to begging.

"The movie isn't real, but that doesn't mean enemies can't become friends in real life. Some even fall in love. It's not all make-believe. Some things are real."

I learn a lot about Meg from this speech. She knows the movies are fairy tales, but she still believes that the fantasy is real. At least at Christmas time.

I've reached the point where I will play dirty to get out of watching her entertainment of choice. Only a little subterfuge is needed.

"You're right," I say.

"What?"

"You're right. One night isn't enough to change your opinion of me. We need the week."

She shakes her head. "I'm only here for three days."

"Then the next three days."

Her eyes narrow. "Do you expect me to soften toward you in three days?"

"Yes," I say slowly. "I'm not the horrible person you think I am."

She snorts. "You're sure about that?"

"Yep." This is my last-ditch effort to show her I'm a better man than she gives me credit for. “Prove me wrong.”

“That should be easy. How do you suggest I do it?”

“For the next three days, we’ll do holiday activities together.” I point to the TV. “Like they do in these movies you love. If by the time you leave, you soften toward me even a little, then I win. If you still dislike me, then you win.”

She’s shaking her head before I finish speaking. “You don’t like these movies. You already said they were unrealistic. Why would you bet that decorating a tree will soften me toward you?”

“I may not like the movies, but what you said is true. Two people who spend time together come to understand one another. Once an understanding is forged, they can let go of animosity.”

“Or they dislike each other more.”

What is her problem? She is good and kind to everyone but me. Eleven years of loathing is long enough! I swallow my resentment and smile.

“That’s what this bet is about,” I say.

She shakes her head. “I don’t want to make a stupid bet with you.”

“Because you know you’ll lose?”

“Because I have better things to do than spend my time with you.”

I don’t care how much she resents me, watching sappy movies is not better than my company.

“Because you know you’ll lose,” I reiterate.

She doesn’t say anything for a long minute. I stare at her profile.

“If I win,” she says, “Then you have to skip next Christmas with my family.”

She says this like I harass her family, and she's protecting them from me. I have three days to prove her wrong. It's worth the risk.

"Okay."

I must have capitulated too quickly. Her lips press into a line. "Five years of no Christmas with my family."

I can't tell if she wants out of the bet by making this extreme, or if she wants to see how much pain she can inflict on me before I cry "Uncle." I have a high tolerance for emotional pain. She'll be disappointed.

"Two Christmases," I say.

She studies me for a while before she nods in agreement. "Fine. Not that it will happen, but if you win, what do you want?"

If I'm willing to sacrifice so much for the chance to convince her I'm a good person, a little teasing on my part is in order.

"You have to kiss me."

She laughs. Hysterically. "No way! I'd rather lick the bottom of your shoe."

"I'm amenable. Kiss me or lick the bottom of my shoe." Such a comment deserves payback. "For ten—no, twenty seconds."

She laughs harder. "Twenty seconds? You must be delusional. Why would you want to kiss me anyway?"

Because she has extremely kissable lips and the one kiss we shared—before popularity went to my head and destroyed everything—still remains the best kiss I've ever had.

Obviously, I'm not answering that question aloud. "Do we have a deal?"

Chapter Six

MEG

I CAN'T BELIEVE I'M ENTERTAINING THE IDEA OF ENTERING THIS stupid bet with Noah. Just contemplating spending time with him threatens to give me hives. We tried that eleven years ago, and he broke my heart.

And a kiss? Yuck. Not that I have anything to worry about. There is no way I will ever soften toward him. I've already won. The next two Christmases without Noah? A done deal.

But why would he even want to kiss me after he ghosted me the last time we kissed? This whole situation is ridiculous. He must be desperate for something to do over the next few days if he's willing to spend so much time with me to win a kiss he doesn't want.

I know spending time together won't soften me toward him, but it gives me a chance to make him miserable. It's been a long time since Noah and I were friends, but I still know him. I know exactly how to torture him. That would definitely make me the winner and be worth sacrificing a few hours in his presence.

My silence makes Noah squirm, so I let him stew for another long minute before saying, "Why are we doing this?"

"I want a chance to prove I'm not the terrible person you think I am."

"But why do you care what I think of you? You haven't cared in eleven years. Why now?"

"I've always cared." Sincerity rings in his words.

"Then why haven't you done anything about it sooner?" I'm honestly curious.

He tilts his head to the side and purses his lips. "I'm doing something about it now."

"By making me do Christmas movie stuff with you over the next few days?"

"Exactly."

"You know this is ridiculous, right?"

"No, I don't. I think it sounds fun. Besides, don't you want to live inside your own Christmas movie?"

He has a point. Wasn't I the one who compared Livy's situation to a movie? Aren't I the one who's pushing her to consider a stranger she met on the side of the road as a viable love interest because that's what happens in the movies?

Out loud, I say, "Have you ever heard of entertainment for the sake of being entertained?"

"Well, think of the next three days as entertainment. I'm out to prove that Christmas activities can bring two enemies to an understanding in real life. You're out to prove me wrong."

His eyes glow with eagerness. He really wants to do this.

"If you never watch the movies," I say, "How would you know what they do in them?"

"I watched a few tonight. They built a snowman, decorated a tree, gathered donations for an orphanage, and had an awkward moment under the mistletoe. I think I can figure it out. Also, Google."

I squash down my smile. This is getting even more ridiculous. "So, like, one thing a day we'll do together?"

"Uh, no. That leaves way too much time for you to subject me to more of," he waves at the TV. "That. I don't want brain rot. Five things a day."

My jaw drops. "Five? That's excessive."

His brow raises, and there's an evil glint in his eyes. "Five from each of us."

"Ten activities every day? Together?" This is so much worse than I thought.

"Yep."

"Six," I counter.

"Ten." He leans closer to me.

"Seven."

"Twelve." That evil glint has turned into merriment.

"That isn't how negotiations work. We meet in the middle. You can't go higher."

"Fifteen."

I abhor how much I enjoy his playful side. It reminds me too much of our year of friendship. We squabbled like this all the time.

"Eighteen." His smile turns to a gloat.

"Fine. Ten, " I say. It will give more more opportunities to torture him. "I will plan five activities for tomorrow. We'll take turns. But what if someone doesn't want to participate in an activity chosen by the other person?"

"They have to, or they forfeit."

"What happens in the case of a forfeit?"

"The other person wins."

"Perfect." And it really is. When I get him to give up, I'll have two Noah free Christmases. "Our bet starts tomorrow. I want to finish my movie tonight."

"You're sitting on my bed," he says. "If you'd like, I'm happy to take your room and you can sleep out here. Otherwise, I'd appreciate it if you'd vacate the couch."

He has a point. I have a Christmas movie app on my phone. I prefer watching on the larger screen, but it'll be good enough for tonight.

"Fine." I stand and stalk past him, but wonder why they didn't request another bed. It would be more comfortable than sleeping on a couch. "Is this where you slept last night? Why don't you get an extra bed from housekeeping?"

"Matt snores. I'd rather be out here. Last night, I slept in your bed."

Yuck. As if things aren't terrible enough, he has to contaminate my bedroom.

"Did you change the sheets, or at least ask for new ones?" I ask.

He gives me a sheepish look. "I didn't think about it."

Now I get to stew in Noah's germs all night. I stomp out of the living room, muttering about his selfishness, loud enough to be heard.

Chapter Seven

NOAH

AFTER A LONG SHOWER SUNDAY MORNING, I'M PULLING ON jeans when I realize I forgot to grab a shirt. I rub the towel through my hair as I enter the living room and head to my suitcase. I don't get far because Meg is camped out on the couch wearing sleep shorts and a skin-tight tank top. She's always been curvy, and there is a lot of skin on display. Like, a lot. For a second, I struggle to look up at her face.

She glances over, and the spoon full of cereal pauses halfway to her mouth. She's mixed ice cream and a smidge of milk in with her Fruit Loops. Her favorite breakfast. Her eyes widen as they take in my chest.

I recover first, but instead of heading to my open suitcase, I stand right where I am and fold my arms, showing off my biceps to their advantage. Her cheeks turn pink.

A hoodie lies next to her on the couch, but I can understand why she isn't wearing it. The gas fireplace is on full blast and the room is sweltering. I much prefer cold temperatures. Apparently, Meg doesn't agree.

Of course, another Christmas movie is playing. The woman speaking on screen has an obnoxious, high-pitched voice. I'm guessing she's not the love interest, but some evil ex. Someone in the movie drops a pan, and Meg startles, breaking her eye contact with my bare skin.

"Did you leave any hot water?" Her voice is too high. She clears her throat. "You were in there for a long time."

"The water was hot when I turned it off. I'm sure you'll be fine. We're starting our bet today. Christmas movies are not on the agenda."

She smiles with dastardly delight. "But they are." She waves to the TV. "A movie is our first activity, but this one is over soon so it doesn't count. You get to sit here for two full hours and watch the next one. While I take a shower. My bed smells like your nasty cologne, and now I smell like it too."

Many women have commented on how much they like my cologne. I quite like it myself. I feel bad about not changing the sheets, but she's making a big deal out of very little.

"You can't take a shower while I watch a movie," I say. "The point is to do stuff together. It doesn't count if you leave me alone."

She rolls her eyes. "So nit-picky. It's not like me sitting on the couch while watching a movie is going to change my opinion of you."

"If I have to suffer, so do you. And each activity can only be used once. I'm not watching five movies today. Or any other movie for the next few days."

"Whatever," she huffs.

I turn to the kitchen to grab a bowl and fill it with wheat Chex cereal. I drown it in milk. No ice cream for me.

"Have you checked on your parents?" I ask.

"Of course." She sounds offended I would imply otherwise.

"How are they?"

"About the same. They really got something bad at that taco stand. They need rest and liquids, but I think they'll feel better by Christmas Eve."

I sit on the couch opposite Meg.

"Can you please put on a shirt before you get settled?" Meg says just as I get settled. She points in my general direction without actually looking. "No one wants to see *that* first thing in the morning. Definitely not me."

Liar. I noticed how she ogled me. I stay right where I am and glance down at my chest, pretending to look for something that would warrant her wrinkled nose. I work out at hotel gyms wherever I end up. I spend time in the sun. I fill out a shirt well. I'm sure she agrees. Either way, I'm not putting on a shirt. I'm sweating, with the fireplace turned up so high.

"You're a nurse," I say. "I'm sure you see a lot of bare chests."

"None that I'm not paid to deal with."

"So, no boyfriend, eh?"

Her eyes narrow. "None of your business."

"You're not much more clothed than I am."

"Whatever."

I hate that word. She had a friend in high school who said, "Whatever," to everything. It drove me crazy.

Meg's bare skin is having the same effect on me as my chest has on her. Could she not find a tank top a size larger? I'm surprised she could get this one over her ... head.

We eat our breakfast while the couple on the screen proclaim their love for each other and kiss. Meg smiles like this is the best moment in cinematic history, but it's overacted and excessively sentimental.

She glances over and catches my scowl. It makes her laugh. It's worth the torture to hear the sound. I haven't seen carefree Meg in a long time.

"You might surprise yourself and love the next one," she says.

"I wouldn't bet on it."

"Right. We bet on much better things than movies."

Is that sarcasm? Before I can respond, she jumps off the couch and heads to the kitchen.

"We're also having hot cocoa," she says. "Two activities together."

"You want cocoa when it's already *Furnace Creek* in here?"

I'm roasting from the outside in, and now I get to roast from the inside out? My first activity will be making snow angels outside. Shirtless.

"Cocoa and Christmas movies are synonymous. Deal with it."

Within the first ten minutes of the movie, I can see exactly where this is going. The woman is a poor, struggling mother. The man is an egotistical businessman trying to steal her farm and goes undercover to do it. Boring. I hope this leaves no permanent brain damage.

Meg comes from the kitchen carrying two Styrofoam cups with lids. She holds one out to me.

"Careful, it's hot," she says with a smirk.

I take it with both hands ... to find the cup weighs nothing. I jiggle it a little.

"There's nothing in here."

She situates herself on the couch, hiding her smile behind her own cup. Steam rises from the top slit, evidence that her cup is not empty.

"That's the thing about Christmas movies," she says. "They drink a lot of hot cocoa, but they actually never drink hot cocoa. Their mugs are obviously empty. You're lucky, because I'm giving you a lesson on how to pretend your cup is full of cocoa when it's actually full of air."

I don't want hot cocoa, but I also don't want to pretend my cup isn't full of hot air, kind of like Meg.

"I would rather have the cocoa," I say.

She puts her finger to her lip. "Shush. This is my activity. Now, the first thing you must do is hold the cup like there is weight to it, like so." She holds her cup with both hands and moves it slowly to her lips. "Don't slosh it around or tip it. Hold it steady. Second, sip it. Don't tilt your head back like the cup is half empty already. Also, don't swallow it like a cup of room-temperature water. This is a hot drink from a full cup."

She demonstrates her lesson by taking the tiniest sip, barely tilting her cup back.

"Except you have hot cocoa in your cup," I point out.

"Or I'm an excellent actor."

"Or you're full of crap."

She laughs again. I could grow addicted to the sound. It's like bells and makes me think of the ending of *It's a*

Wonderful Life, my grandma's all-time favorite movie. *Every time Meg laughs, an angel gets his wings.*

"Go ahead," she says encouragingly. "Show me your acting skills."

She's really enjoying this lesson, and it's kind of nice not having her cold shoulder. So, I do as she requests. I lift my cup like there's something inside, blow on the top gently, then tilt it the tiniest bit and take a tentative sip of air.

When I look over at Meg, she has a peculiar look on her face and she's staring at my mouth.

"What?" I ask. "Do I have whipped cream on my upper lip?"

It's a joke, but she suddenly grows serious again. "Of course not. Don't be a twit."

We were having such a great time; it bothers me she's pulling away again. If she can tease, so can I.

"I'm pretty sure I have whipped cream on my upper lip," I say. "Since we're two characters in a movie, I think it's your job to wipe it away."

The scowl is back. "Not a chance. Besides, how would you know that happens in romance movies unless you've watched them before?"

"I may not like Christmas romance movies, but I've seen my fair share of romcoms. There's always an eyelash or a streak of flour on a cheek. In our case, it's cream. On my upper lip. You better get it off."

"No."

"My pick."

She glowers. "You're wasting one of your activities on fake whipped cream? Fine. Let me get a napkin."

"Nope." I put my arm out to stop her from standing. "Use your finger. A napkin isn't movie worthy."

"And wiping fake whipped cream from your lip with my finger is?" If she were standing, her hands would be on her hips.

"Try it and you tell me. I've only ever seen it on a screen."

Her face scrunches up and she reaches out tentatively. "Ew, ew, ew, ew, ew."

I don't even have anything on my lip but air, and she's still grossed out.

I'm about to call off the joke since my ego is still recovering from yesterday, but then her thumb touches the corner of my mouth. Both of us go rigid at the contact. Her thumb slowly traverses my upper lip. Her eyes catch mine and for three seconds neither of us look away.

I may be having a heart attack, but I'm not concerned because this moment is perfect. Maybe romance movies know what they're talking about. Sometimes.

Meg drops her hand and leans as far from me as she can. "Two activities for me, one for you. Now shut up. This is a good part."

I swallow down my desire to pull Meg close and feel more of her skin against mine. We're both half-dressed. It might push my alleged heart attack into cardiac arrest, but it could be worth it.

No, it wouldn't. She detests me. Touching her might lead to my homicide. I don't want to put her in jail for the next fifty years.

I resist her siren call and try for the same disinterested attitude she puts out. "This is another one you've seen before, and you're still making me watch it?"

"I told you. It's a good one."

"A good, romantic Christmas movie is like Big Foot. It doesn't exist. Unless it's a classic. Can't we watch *Elf* instead?"

"*Elf* is not a classic." She hides a tiny smile by taking another sip of real hot cocoa. "Be quiet."

Right. I sit back and try to watch the movie, but it doesn't do much to distract me from Meg. It doesn't help that the plot is even more contrived than I originally suspected.

Chapter Eight

MEG

NOAH SITS THROUGH THE REST OF THE MOVIE WITHOUT SAYING another word. I expect snide comments galore, or for him to take a really long bathroom break, but he sits and watches quietly. Sometimes he grimaces at the stuff that happens on screen, and I take silent pleasure in his pain. Especially after that stunt with the whipped cream.

Touching him felt ... nice. I don't want to feel nice around Noah. He's my enemy. There will be no Christmas magic happening between us.

Still, I hardly pay attention to the movie. It's one I've seen many times, and shirtless Noah takes up too much space in my brain to focus on anything else. Every time I take a swallow of my cocoa, he pretends to sip from his empty cup. With each swallow, he tips the cup back just a bit more until he reaches the bottom and leans his head back all the way. He even taps the side of the cup to get the last few invisible drops. He could give these actors a few pointers on how to make fake hot cocoa drinking more realistic.

He's being a good sport about the movie and the empty cup. It's fun. Noah and I always had fun together when we were friends. Something I don't want to think about. Ever. When I do, I'm swallowed by a feeling of loss so deep I can't find the bottom.

The moment the credits roll, he grabs the remote and turns off the TV.

"And you actually enjoy watching those?" he asks.

Maybe not the movie we just watched. It's one of the stupider stories. The characters are excessively cliche, the acting isn't great, and the plot is even more predictable than usual. I could have found a better movie, but this bet isn't about superior entertainment. It's about torture. And maybe a smidge to do with revenge.

"It was fantastic. Right?" I say with a huge smile.

He just stares, expression incredulous, and I laugh. I don't want to laugh because I don't want him to think I enjoy spending time with him. I'm not. His eyes study my face, and my smile slips away. The moment feels charged. With what, I can't say. Definitely not attraction.

Time for a break. I stand. "I need to check on my family."

The hallway is downright chilly after the sweltering heat of the main room, and I rub my arms.

My parents' light is off, and the curtains are drawn. I wait until my eyes adjust to the dimness before I take any steps past the door. Dad stirs.

"Hey, sweetie." His voice is soft, but not weak.

"How does your stomach feel? Are you still nauseous?"

He groans. "Yeah, but better than yesterday."

I look at the glass of water on his nightstand. He hasn't had any since I checked in earlier.

"You have to drink fluids, Dad. We don't want you to get dehydrated."

"It makes me want to throw up."

"At least try."

I go around the bed to Mom.

"Sweet Meg." She doesn't sound as miserable as Dad. "I could actually use more water."

"Sure. Are you up for some broth?"

They both groan out a no. I refill her glass in the bathroom sink and lay more Pepto Bismol tablets on their nightstands.

"I'm so sorry to ruin your Christmas," Mom says. "I thought this would be a nice surprise, but you'd be having fun with your roommates if it weren't for us."

Maybe. Or I would be alone because Livy went to her sister's in Wyoming, and Layla's in Maine with her fiancé. I'd rather be here taking care of my family, even if that means spending a few days with Noah.

"I'm glad you came," I say. "Can I get you anything else?"

"No, we're fine." She pats my hand. "You should go out and do something. No reason for you to be cooped up here all day because of us."

"Actually, Noah and I have some plans. You're sure it's okay if we leave you alone?"

"Of course." She groans and sits up. "Excuse me."

She gets out of bed and disappears into the bathroom.

"Go on," Dad says. "Go do your thing. We're okay."

I wish there was something more I could do to help them, but food poisoning just needs to run its course.

"Promise you'll text me if you need anything," I say.

"Will do," he says.

I head to Matt's room.

"Finally," he says. "I need more water."

I grab his water bottle. "Sure. Give me a sec."

When I get back from filling it in the bathroom, he asks, "Is Noah still here?"

Unfortunately. "Yeah."

He takes a swallow of water. "I thought you might have scared him off."

Wouldn't that be lovely.

"He can go spend Christmas with his mom or dad," I say, even knowing that isn't an option. While we were friends, he told me they cared more about winning the most in the divorce than they did about him. That hasn't changed if I had to judge by how much time he spends with my family.

"Don't frighten him away," Matt says.

"This isn't a horror movie. What do you think I'm going to do? Chase after him with a chainsaw?"

"You know how you were with him in high school. Clingy. You embarrassed him. Just keep your distance now, and he won't feel the need to flee."

My chest feels tight. I leave Matt's room without another word and take a breather in the hallway.

Clingy. An embarrassment. The words echo in my head. That wasn't all Noah said about me after he made the baseball team and had half the female student body chasing after him. Matt told me Noah shared with the team and anyone who would listen that I was a terrible kisser, drew hearts in the place of periods (is that a crime?), and still loved my Furby (he was cute).

Tonight Matt's warning is a good reminder that Noah isn't to be trusted. My friendship with him is long over. All I'm worried about now is the future. Preferably with Noah finding somewhere else to spend Christmas for the next two years.

When I come back into the living room, Noah's kneeling at the coffee table looking through the box of tree decorations Mom brought. Christmas carols play on his phone. The holidays don't mean much to him, so I'm surprised he thought to turn it on.

"We're decorating the tree?" I ask, though the answer is obvious.

"Yep," he says. "Judy brought popcorn for us to string into a garland and ingredients for gingerbread cookies. We can make those three different activities if you want?"

That's decent, instead of forcing me to do all three for one activity. I shrug like it's no big deal. "Whatever."

I stand near the couch, unwilling to move closer, feeling awkward now that I have to spend time with him when the TV isn't involved. What are we supposed to talk about? Or will we move around each other, stuck in unpleasant silence? At least he's put on a shirt. It's white and snug across his shoulders, so I'm not sure it helps. My eyes keep veering down past his face.

"I've never decorated a tree before," he continues. "How do you want to do this?"

"Never?" I ask incredulously. "You had a Christmas tree growing up."

"My Mom always decorated it after I went to bed on Christmas Eve. She liked doing it alone and having it up for only a few days. I never had a tree when I lived with my dad."

I did not know this. It's sad, and I feel myself softening toward him. *Softening is not allowed. Toughen up, Meg!*

"Just stick the ornaments wherever," I say.

"No preference?"

"Nope. Just have fun."

"Fun I can do." He points to the counter. "I made you a sandwich."

I am hungry and not about to turn down food, even if it comes from my enemy. Again. I sit at the table and watch him decorate while I eat. He toasted the bread how I like it, and the cheese is melted just enough to mix with the ranch dressing. Delicious.

He's a much better sandwich maker than a tree decorator. He doesn't appear to have spatial awareness because he's hung all the silver balls in a clump. The shape of them reminds me of a cloud. It looks stupid, but I said I didn't care, so now I have to stick by those words. I just didn't expect him to be so terrible at such a simple activity.

"I googled Christmas romance movies," he says. He's been busy while I've been checking on my family. "Did you know playing Hallmark bingo while watching a movie is a thing?"

"I did know that."

"Have you ever played?"

"No," I lie. I've convinced Livy and Layla to play a few times.

"Apparently, it's common for characters to write wishes and hang them on the tree. I found some stationery in the desk. I thought we could write a wish down, fold them into origami stars, and put them in the tree."

I've never placed a wish on a tree, but it does happen in a lot of movies. It's probably more effective than wishing on a planet.

"Whatever."

Noah grimaces.

He leaves the tree to grab a pen and a piece of paper he's cut into a perfect pentagon. He hands them to me.

"How did you get this shape so perfect?" I ask.

"I like origami. Just one of the tricks of the trade."

I remember. During class, it helped him concentrate to have his fingers busy with something while he listened. He would write me notes, fold them into origami shapes, and slip them into my locker. I wonder if I still have those somewhere.

He sits opposite me at the table and scribbles out a wish before deftly making some folds. Suddenly, he has a star. Cool trick.

I focus on my wish. My wish from two nights ago isn't possible anymore. Noah's crashed Christmas. Matt's sick. There is no bridging the gap between me and my brother this year.

In my loopiest cursive, I write, *I wish to torture Noah until I win this bet*. I make sure to put hearts above every "i."

When I look up, Noah's waiting for me to hand him my paper. I'm not sure I want to and pull my wish closer. If he sees my wish, it won't come true.

"I won't peek," he says. "I promise."

"How do I know I can trust you?"

"Because if I peek, then your wish won't come true. I want your wish to come true."

He wouldn't if he knew what I wrote.

"Google is really detailed about movie traditions," I say.

"Lucky for me." His hand is still outstretched toward me.

Still, I hesitate. "How do you plan not to peek if you're folding the star?"

"I'll close my eyes. I once made one thousand origami stars for a friend's birthday party. Believe me, I can fold without peeking."

I'm not sure I trust him, but I also know I don't want to sit close enough for him to teach me how to fold my own. I slide it over, and as promised, he closes his eyes and makes the folds. He moves slower than with his own wish, but not by much.

Once done, he slides it back across the table and both of us go to hang our wishes on the tree. His goes prominently above his silver cloud. I hide mine on the opposite side, so far in that pine needles hide the small white star. I don't trust Noah not to peek at my wish when I'm not around.

Noah goes back to hanging balls in clumps, and I look through the box of ornaments Mom brought. At home, she puts up three artificial trees on November first and doesn't take them down until mid-January. Each tree has a different theme, and every ornament has a place.

But Mom also believes decorating can be a form of artistic expression, so while we grew up, she set up a tree in each of our rooms so that we could decorate them any way we wanted. Matt decided having a Christmas tree in his bedroom was lame right around sixth grade. I kept mine until I went away to college.

And here are all those decorations from both of our trees. It's like a genealogical dig. Matt's Star Wars ornaments and my Winnie the Pooh ones from when we were kids. The year I went with a nautical theme. In high school, I was all about the traditional Santa faces, reindeer, and snowmen. I had no idea she kept these, and the fact she did makes me inordinately happy.

Noah's decorating the left side of the tree, so I take the right. I trip over a gift box that slipped out from underneath. It's my gift to Noah, and I kick it back under until it stays.

I sent my presents to Idaho Falls weeks ago and my parents brought them back. Mom and Dad expect Noah and me to exchange gifts, so we usually give each other something small. This year, I bought him dress socks with a gaudy Christmas pattern. He will hate them.

Neither of us speaks as we decorate. With the Christmas music playing, it's peaceful. And what is there not to love about decorating a tree? We have lights, the pine scent, colorful decorations, and memories. I wish my parents and Matt were here to help. There would be conversation and laughter. Since it's just Noah and me, I'll take the silence.

Once Noah has used every ball ornament, he goes to the kitchen and heats up oil for popping corn. I glance at my watch.

"We only have ninety minutes for the garland," I tell him. "My activity starts at two." I suppress my cackle. I don't want to give anything away. Matt told me not to embarrass Noah, so I plan to do exactly that.

"Will we be done by five?" he asks. "We have reservations at Quest downstairs."

My mouth literally drops open. "You got dinner reservations at Quest this close to Christmas?"

He shrugs like it's no big deal, but it's a big deal. They're always booked out months.

"I know a guy," he says. "But not that great of a guy. Five is early for dinner, but it's the only time he could get us in."

"This isn't a date."

"No, it's a movie activity." He doesn't miss a beat. "I'm positive they eat in movies."

I've always wanted to go to Quest, but it's freaking expensive. An entree is at least fifty dollars, which will blow up my food budget this month, but it will be worth it.

"Okay," I say, "But I'm paying for myself."

"They already have my credit card. Sorry, my pick. I pay."

I see the wisdom of making my enemy pay for an expensive meal. I hope they have lobster.

Noah pops the popcorn at the stove and the scent permeates the air. When I've placed my last ornament perfectly, I take a step back to enjoy the beauty. It's a little bit of every style of ornament from my childhood. I love it.

It's obvious there is no cohesion between our two halves, but it has a certain charm. Until I move to the left and take in all the ball ornaments. Noah's silver cloud hangs over two green eyes, a huge, bulbous red nose, a red slash that can only be lips, and a green bowtie.

"What do you think of my clown?" he asks.

"It's awful." I have to work to suppress my laughter. It is awful, but hilarious as well. I try for a severe tone of voice. "Like every other sane human on earth, I hate clowns. Why would you put one on the tree?"

I glance over my shoulder and see the huge grin Noah's

trying to hide. I must not be the only person in this bet who is going for torture. I swear there's a twinkle in his eye.

"You said you didn't care," he says.

"Apparently, I do."

He can't contain his mirth a second longer and he laughs. I bite down on my smile. Well played, Noah. Well played.

"Come help with the garland?" he asks.

While he fills a few bowls with popcorn, I thread fishing wire through needles and tie off the ends. Then we're sitting together at the table, stringing popcorn. It isn't as easy as I assumed. More kernels crumble in my hand than make it on the line.

As for Noah, he keeps poking his fingertips with the needle. Each time he does he sucks a breath through his teeth. A few drops of red mar the white popcorn. It's painful to watch *and* listen to.

"Stop eating the popcorn," he says.

"I'm just trying to move this along. If we string every one of these kernels, we'll be here all day. We have to leave in twenty-five minutes to get to our next activity."

His shoulders slump as he looks over the bowls of popcorn. He's torturing himself, and I did nothing but show up for it. It's delightful.

"You're right." He grabs a handful of popcorn and stuffs it into his mouth. "It tastes a lot better than it looks strung up anyway."

I follow his lead. When both of our cheeks are puffed out like chipmunks, we burst out laughing. Half-chewed kernels shoot out of my mouth, which makes him laugh harder.

I still don't like him though.

Chapter Nine

NOAH

AFTER STICKING THREE VERY SHORT STRANDS OF POPCORN ON the tree, Meg checks on her family and changes into jeans and a hoodie. Thank goodness. I wasn't sure how much longer I could keep myself from staring at her bare legs.

She leads me down to the second floor, where the lodge has a community room.

A sign hangs outside the double doors that reads, "Welcome to Santa's Workshop!" in funky, playful lettering.

We step through and join a line of people waiting to check in at the front desk. I glance around. There are four booths staffed by employees dressed in green sweaters and red Santa hats. I'm guessing they're elves since this is Santa's workshop. Each table has a sign with a picture of a craft.

Cheesy, annoying Christmas music blares.

Kids run around wildly or sit at the tables. The few

adults in attendance sit on the chairs around the perimeter of the room, looking at their phones.

Meg brought us to the wrong place.

I lean close and whisper in her ear. "These are kids' crafts."

"Embarrassed?" she says with a note of challenge in her voice.

Okay, so this is on purpose.

"I don't think Christmas movies have couples doing kids' crafts," I say. At least I hope not.

"They do if I say they do. I dare you to prove otherwise." She leans closer until her arm is flush with mine. I like it more than I should. "Or do you want to forfeit and make me the victor?"

My competitive spirit rises. Make crafts with little kids? Sure. "I'm game."

"We'll see. My activity choice is to do all four."

She doesn't break eye contact, so I don't either.

"Is this a craft competition?" I ask. "Are you judging my effort afterward?"

"Mmmm ... I think I will. You have to at least try or it's a forfeit."

Before I can comment on this new rule, we make it to the front table, where the elf holds a clipboard. She has blinking Christmas lights hanging around her neck and a name tag that reads "Eve." The name tag is in the shape of Santa's head, with his hat, beard, and red circle cheeks. What's missing is his actual face. No eyes, lips, or nose, just a name scrawled across like a huge tattoo. It's kind of creepy.

"Name?" Eve asks.

"Meg Wright," Meg says.

"You paid for two children to do all four crafts today?" She looks around our legs, probably expecting two kids to materialize from behind us.

"Close." Meg points to herself and then to me. "We're the two doing the crafts."

Confusion creases her forehead. "Oh. Okay?"

"Your website didn't mention any age restrictions."

Meg is unapologetic for crashing a kids' activity. She's more confident than she was in high school. I'm the one who feels uncomfortable. Kids have always made me feel out of my element. And crafts? My patience extends to folding paper.

The elf chews her lip for a few seconds, debating. "I guess that's okay." She hands over two red plastic wristbands.

Meg grins like she won a major battle on two fronts and leads the way to our first station. There's a skip in her step. I didn't realize she enjoyed crafting this much.

Meg tugs me down to sit in a child-sized chair. Her knees rise a few inches higher than her hips. My knees are up to my chin. Like I needed another reason to feel out of place.

We take ninety minutes to complete our first three crafts: a gnome ornament, a small glass jar snow globe, and a mini wreath out of a Mason jar lid ring and strips of material. Or I should say, it takes Meg ninety minutes. If I were alone, I would've been done in ten.

The more impatient I get, the slower she goes. After a full, white gnome beard has grown on my chin, she finally, slowly, ties the last knot on the jar ring.

One craft to go. I drag her over. The sign reads, "Ugly Christmas T-shirts contest." The wall behind is full of

Polaroid pictures of ugly T-shirts, and each has a number next to it. Huh. A nice twist on ugly sweaters.

"Those are really ugly," Meg whispers. "Do you think you can make an uglier one?"

"Without even trying."

The T-shirts are in children's sizes. Meg picks a red extra-large. She'll need it that big to get it over her, um ... head. I take the largest size available. I don't think it will fit, at least not well, but I'll give it a try.

This time, instead of sitting, I opt to kneel beside Meg.

"Are you sure you don't want a chair?" Meg asks.

"I'm sure."

"Too bad. You looked ridiculous, and I quite enjoyed the spectacle."

Meg collects items from baskets of supplies on the table. An iron-on of the Grinch's face, a silver tree garland, and child sized-mittens. I'm not sure what she's doing with those, but I'm curious to find out.

I'm not creative like Meg, or carefree like these kids. They'll stick anything on a shirt. Without instructions, I don't know how to start. The only artsy thing I know is folding paper. Maybe the skill is transferable?

One of the baskets is labeled "Felt" and has sturdy material inside. I grab a yellow piece and fold it into an origami star. It looks decent, as long as I don't let go.

I let the star unfold and trim the felt so the edges are clean before I move to the end of the table where the elf named Holly is guarding the hot glue gun like it's a treasure.

"Can I get some glue?" I ask.

"Sure." She picks up the glue gun. "Where do you want it?"

From her fierce expression, I'm sure she won't let me glue it myself, so I make the first few folds and tell her where to add a dot of glue. By the time we're done, I have a decent-looking star. I grab more felt from the basket and start creating something I think is pretty cool.

Chapter Ten

MEG

NOELLE, THE ELF, WILL NOT LET ME USE THE CLOTHES IRON.

"My boss said no one can touch the iron except for me," she says with a scowl.

"You're saying Santa is a control freak? I never would have guessed."

Noelle does not think I'm funny. Arguing isn't getting me anywhere, so I give in and tell her where I want the Grinch's face attached to my shirt.

Next, I have a battle with Mary over the glue gun. Noah is over on the other side of the table, flirting with a different elf who has a second glue gun. They've all been given the same instructions because I have to point to every spot I want the glue.

I cut down the silver tree garland into strips long enough to make a stickman's body, with legs and arms. Mary glues down only the ends of the strips, so the middle parts move when I shake the shirt.

Last, she glues the mittens at the end of the Grinch's garland arms, up above his head.

I'm pleased with what I've created. I hold the shirt up and wiggle it. The Grinch looks cool, dancing to Christmas music. It's ugly, but it also has charm.

I look for Noah so we can head out. I've gone as slow as I can, but two hours has taken all of my patience.

When I spot Noah, he doesn't look ready to leave, which is surprising. He was bored to death with the last three crafts. I made sure of it.

His shirt isn't ugly, either. He pieced together a Christmas tree out of different shades of green felt and even folded the pieces to make the tree look three-dimensional. As I watch, Holly the elf puts a dollop of hot glue at the tiptop of the tree, and he attaches a yellow 3D star.

Kids watch him work; their own shirts forgotten. Noah doesn't notice the fascination he's attracted at his skill of turning an ugly T-shirt into a work of art. He doesn't even notice the three female staff members ogling him.

"Will you make one of those stars for me?" a child asks. She's the cutest little girl, probably six. If I were Noah, I wouldn't be able to say no.

Her question breaks his trance, and he leans back to take in the attention he's garnered.

"Me, too?" a boy asks.

Then Noah's bombarded with queries for stars. As they push toward him, I'm pushed away. A glance at the clock on the wall tells me we have dinner in just over an hour, and it's a swanky place. I need time to get ready, and I haven't showered yet today. I still reek of Noah's cologne. Before Quest, I also need to make dinner for my family.

I don't want to interrupt Noah's fan club, so I give him one last look before I head to the door. He has a friendly innocence that draws people to him. It once drew me in, but never again. It doesn't matter what a good sport he's been today, or how nice he's being to those kids.

I don't trust him.

Noah doesn't notice when I leave. It's a familiar feeling to be ignored by him, so why does it bother me so much this time?

FIFTEEN MINUTES BEFORE OUR DINNER RESERVATION, I'M READY to go. My hair is curled, my makeup is done. I even shaved my legs.

I swirl in front of the bedroom mirror in my pink wrap-around dress with matching heels. It would be more appropriate to a Christmas movie if I wore red, but I look terrible in red.

It's been a while since I've last been somewhere nice and had an excuse to dress up. I brought the dress for Christmas eve dinner, and I'm glad I did. How embarrassing to show up at Quest in jeans and a T-shirt.

Tonight, I mean to enjoy myself, even with Noah. Quest is not the place to hold a grudge. I call a temporary mental truce where I will be on my best behavior and enjoy every bite of food. Afterward, my war on Noah will continue.

Noah knocks on my bedroom door, and I put on a last layer of lipstick before opening it.

I expect to find him in a suit.

I should know by now to expect the unexpected where Noah is concerned.

He's wearing jeans. Nice jeans, so dark they look almost black, but still jeans. And his ugly T-shirt.

The T-shirt really is too small. It's tight on his biceps and snug across his chest. It's barely long enough to cover his belt loops. Since I left him at the North Pole crafternoon, he's attached small beads as ornaments to his tree. Silver, red, and green to resemble his clown face in the living room.

He poses with hands on hips and a huge grin on his face. I turn away to grab a sweater so he can't see me smile. I kind of love it, but I refuse to give him the feedback he obviously craves.

"Why did you leave?" he asks. "One second you were there, and then you were gone. I got overrun by children. I could have used your help."

"We're going to Quest. I had to get ready." I slip on my sweater. "I need to check on Matt and give him dinner. He was asleep earlier when I checked on my parents."

That'll give Noah time to change after his little fashion show in the hallway.

"We'll leave right after," he says. "They don't hold reservations for longer than ten minutes."

"Even if you know a guy?"

He smiles. "Even if you know a guy."

Which makes me wonder who he knows and how. Noah's job has never stationed him in Salt Lake. My mom would have told me if he had been in the area so I could visit. Honestly, she and dad would have driven up to see him. Matt too.

"How do you know this guy?" I ask.

"He lived down the hall from me and Matt in college."

So no one I would know.

I pass Noah, go into the kitchen, and grab a bowl from the cupboard. I dollop mashed potatoes into the bottom and pour over chicken broth. Growing up, this is what Mom made us when we were sick. There's comfort in even just the smell.

I push into Matt's room slowly, not wanting to spill. The bedside lamp is on and Matt lays on his side scrolling on his phone. He looks up as I enter.

"What did you bring me?" he asks as he sits up.

I hand him the bowl. "Mashed potatoes and broth."

He takes a big whiff and smiles until he looks a little closer. "There's no chicken in this?"

"You obviously feel better, but your stomach is still sensitive. I don't think you're ready for solid foods."

Like a child, he groans. "I'm starving."

"If you keep this down, and it doesn't make you nauseous, there's more on the stove."

He slurps up a spoonful. "I'll text you when I want more."

I'm not sure how Matt survives on his own without Mom or me taking care of him.

"Feel free to let me know," I say, "But you'll be waiting a long time if you expect me to deliver it to you."

"Why?"

"Because I'll be at Quest." I spin in a circle to show off my new dress. It has the best twirly skirt.

Matt doesn't appreciate the little performance. His eyes narrow. "With Noah?" His words sound accusatory.

"So?"

He does his trademark sigh, letting me know he thinks I'm stupid. "You shouldn't go with him anywhere, Meg. He probably doesn't leave behind a girlfriend in every city, but he's left enough for me to worry about you."

He's worried about me because of *Noah*? It's like Matt doesn't know who I am. Considering we haven't had a proper conversation in years, he probably doesn't.

"It's food," I say. "Noah and I aren't even friends. You've told me since high school what a player he is. Don't worry."

With his free hand, Matt waves to my outfit. "Then why did you dress up as if you are hoping for more than friendship?"

"Because I'm going to dinner at *Quest*. It has nothing to do with Noah."

"You liked him in high school. Stay away from him now, or you might fall again. I don't want to see you get hurt."

Matt's worry makes it hard to take offense at his bringing up the past again. He knows I don't like talking about what happened when I was stupid and naïve. Still, my plans are not Matt's business. I have no worries about falling in love with Noah and this is dinner at Quest. I'm not missing it.

"Okay," I say to appease him.

When I enter the living area, Noah stands from the couch. He's still wearing the ugly shirt.

"Why didn't you change? You can't show up like that."

He looks down at himself as if he's confused on why I'd say something about his chosen attire. "We're at a ski resort. Quest may be expensive, but they don't have a dress code. People show up wearing all sorts of stuff, usually ski gear. I won't stand out."

"And you know what people wear at Quest because ..."

"I've eaten there a lot over the years."

I take a step back. He's been to Nordquest before? "When?"

He hesitates for a few seconds while he scratches his cheek. "Every February when Matt and I come here to ski."

His words are a physical blow, and I gasp at the pain. My eyes gather tears, and I try to blink them away.

Matt and Noah come here every winter to ski and not once has Matt contacted me. I understand he thinks I don't like to ski, but he can't even call and set up a time for us to get together for dinner? Here I thought that he never visited Salt Lake because he had no reason to. But he has had a reason: skiing. It's one thing when I'm overlooked from Idaho Falls, quite another when he has to pass my apartment to drive up the mountain.

This is Noah's fault. It has to be. What other explanation is plausible?

I walk past Noah and out the condo door into the hallway.

"Meg?"

I have so much pent-up hurt I need to keep moving. I skip the elevator and take the stairs. Noah, being the annoyance he is, follows behind. My heels clatter on the cement steps. His pounding steps echo behind me. He keeps talking, like a yappy dog.

"Meg, I thought you knew."

I'm supposed to believe that? I trusted him once, and he dropped me like garbage. I trust nothing he says.

"I'm sorry," he says. "I didn't know Matt kept our trips from you. Are you angry with me?"

I'm always angry at Noah. Another two days and I will have the two Christmases without him. That is a goal to work toward.

When we arrive at the restaurant, the maître d' shows us to our table. Noah was right. There are people in ski wear, but the majority wear dresses or suits. And most of those people are looking at Noah. He doesn't notice because he's still trying to get my attention.

Once we sit, I hide behind the menu.

He clears his throat loudly.

I don't peek from my hiding place.

"Meg? I thought you were too busy at the hospital to come and see us. That's what Matt made me believe."

Why would Matt lie to me? He has no reason. This is Noah's fault. Like usual.

I'm desperately close to tears, so I don't move the menu. I say, "Okay."

"Yeah? You forgive me?"

This is supposed to be a nice dinner. I wanted to enjoy myself, so even though it's hard, I concede. For now.

"I forgive you." For as long as dinner lasts.

He pauses a beat. "You look very nice tonight."

His compliment shouldn't mean anything to me, they're just words.

"Thank you. You look ridiculous."

"Thank you," he says with a laugh.

The menu wants to lower an inch so I can watch him smile, but I hold it where it is and try to get control of my emotions.

The server arrives with water glasses and takes our order. I haven't looked at the options offered on the menu as I've been too busy feeling hurt, so I ask for the first thing my eyes land on: shepherd's pie.

The server holds out his hand for my menu, and I reluctantly hand it over. What I'd like to do is ask for a second menu and prop them both up along the middle of the table so I can pretend I'm eating alone.

"We'll have a bottle of your Beringer Chardonnay," Noah says, "And the seafood appetizer plate. I would like beef Wellington."

"Yes, sir." Our server leaves with a bow of his head.

It's only then I remember I wanted to order the lobster. Darn.

I pick at my cuticles. "That's an expensive appetizer plate." Almost as expensive as my meal. "And an expensive bottle of wine." It's a lot for him to spend on his enemy.

"I like excellent wine. It's worth the price. So, um. You're a nurse?"

"Yep, Captain Obvious. I'm a nurse."

"It's what you always wanted, and you did it."

My cuticle starts to bleed, so I force myself to put my hands in my lap. I still don't look up. "Yep, unlike you and your dreams for the major league. Instead, you tear apart companies and fire hard-working Americans. It must be exhausting."

I don't even have to look up to know that was a bruising blow. But I don't apologize. We're not friends. It's good we both remember that.

"I save companies, Meg. Yes, some employees lose their jobs, but that means more employees get to keep theirs."

"Whatever."

Awkward silence takes root and grows between us. Noah

clears his throat. I rub my finger along the edge of the tablecloth.

Our server finally returns with our appetizers and pours us each a glass of wine. I take a gulp before popping a shrimp fritter into my mouth. I'm sad and want to stuff my face, but the moment the flavors hit my tongue I slow my chew. These fritters are not meant to be eaten like a potato chip. The seared scallops and crab-stuffed mushrooms are just as delicious. This food is incredible.

I'm at Quest, eating this delicious food and drinking buttery wine, and I'm miserable. That has got to be an oxymoron.

I don't understand why Noah kept Matt from telling me he was nearby every year, especially after he's been decent to me today, but that doesn't have to ruin my meal.

I sit up, look up, and hardest of all, smile. Noah brought up a topic I feel comfortable talking about, so I take it as the lifeline it is.

"Yes, I'm a nurse. I really enjoy it. I started a clothing drive a few months ago for people to donate old clothes. Many of our patients live on the streets or have so little, and at times, we have to cut their clothes off. They're left with nothing to wear. It's been an excellent program. I'm happy with how it's going."

I continue to tell him about the hospital, some of my past patients, and my coworkers. Anything to fill the silence and make things normal between us, at least while the meal lasts.

He leans forward, his expression open. I've forgotten how attentive he is as a listener. And those eyes. They pull me in against my will.

I mention how Doctor Doug brings the nurses donuts or cupcakes a few times a month, and how he's a favorite with the patients and staff. After going on about him for a few minutes, I realize I sound love-struck. I'm not, just hopeful, but that is more information than I want Noah to have.

"What about becoming a traveling nurse?" Noah asks. "Wasn't that your ultimate goal?"

When I was a teenager, the idea of working all over the United States was one reason I wanted to be a nurse. Becoming a traveling nurse remained my goal throughout nursing school and into the first year of working the floor, but died when the opportunity to become one presented itself. Going off on my own felt too overwhelming. Scary, even. I stayed in Salt Lake.

I don't know if that was the right decision, but I rarely regret it. As much as I love my independence, I don't enjoy living alone. Even during busy weeks when I barely see my roommates, I know they're there and those few minutes we talk in passing mean a lot to me.

In response to Noah's question, I say, "I like living within a few hours of my parents, and this is where my friends are. Maybe someday."

He nods. "Traveling can be great, but it's also lonely. When I'm not onsite, I can work remotely. I've been to a dozen countries and stayed in every state." His voice is weary.

That's the adventure I crave, but I'd find it lonely, too. That's why I still live here.

"Are you tired of traveling?" I ask.

He shrugs. "Maybe? Coming back to an empty hotel room every day can be depressing. Sometimes I think about buying a house just so I have a place to go home to between clients."

The server brings our meal. My shepherd's pie is served in an individual ramekin. I take my spoon and crack open the buttery crust. It crackles. The inside is fragrant, and filled with potatoes, cheese, and lamb. The creamy sauce is steaming. Everything melts in my mouth.

We eat in silence for a few minutes, both of us appreciating our meal. Oddly enough, Noah eats with his left hand. I'm the lefty, he's right-handed, so it strikes me as weird. Maybe he's ambidextrous now?

"If you decided to buy a house," I ask. "Would it be in Idaho Falls?"

He chews slowly and swallows. "I don't know. Matt and your parents live in Idaho Falls, but my mom is in North Dakota and my dad is in Washington."

"I didn't think you were close with your parents?"

"I'm not, but I visit them both once or twice a year. We go out to dinner. Maybe if I lived closer, we could try for a relationship?"

He sounds forlorn, like the abandoned child he is. I want to selfishly tell him to work on those relationships because then his hold on Matt would loosen, and he might rely less on my parents, and they're *my* parents. But I could give myself the same advice. I'm the one who hasn't visited them in eight months.

I also remember in high school all the times Noah's dad didn't show up to his baseball games. All the times his mom promised to call, but never did. Trying for a relationship with them would be a battle he'd lose. The wounds they've left in him would only grow deeper. I can't encourage that, so I don't say anything.

Noah continues. "Besides not knowing where to settle, I don't want to buy a house if there's no one to come home to. I guess that's why I go to Idaho Falls and stay with Matt so often."

This does not sound like he has girlfriends all over the states. Unless they're casual relationships that are only ever meant to be short-term? The picture Matt sketched over the years of Noah's many conquests is different from the one Noah draws for me of returning to an empty hotel room. Is Noah trying to pull my heartstrings? Because against my will, it's working.

I shouldn't care. Noah's personal life is none of my business, and I'm going to keep it that way.

Chapter Eleven

NOAH

After our rocky beginning, dinner is nice. Meg is chatty and outwardly friendly, but she's leery of me. Her smiles are stiff, and she looks at the other diners more than she looks at me.

Until she found out about the ski trip Matt and I go on with a few friends every year, I thought today was going well. I believed I was making headway in proving I'm not a horrible person.

Now I'm right back where I started.

I can't understand why Matt would lie to me. Every February I ask if we're meeting up with Meg, and every year he tells me she's busy. I thought it was because I was with Matt and she was avoiding me, but now I find out she never even knew.

The server comes and takes our plates and asks if we'd like dessert.

"No, thank you," Meg says.

"I'll have your raspberry chocolate cake." I get one every time I visit. "With two forks."

"One fork," Meg says. "I don't want dessert."

"You might want to try it."

She shakes her head. "I won't."

The cake I'm brought is a two-tiered, perfectly round individual cake with chocolate glaze, a buttercream and raspberry middle, and white chocolate drizzled on top.

Meg's eyes widen. They widen further as I stick my fork into the moist, fluffy cake and then slowly glide it into my mouth.

"Would you like to try it?" I ask after I swallow.

Meg battles the desire, but she can't resist. "Fine. Just a small bite."

I push my plate toward her and offer my fork since she refused one of her own, but she uses the butter knife instead to slice off a sliver.

When she tastes it, her eyes close and her shoulders slump. It's the happiest I've seen her all week.

"This is heavenly," she says in a hushed tone. "How do they do this? Are they magic?"

"Have more."

She ends up eating more than half of the cake. After she scrapes the last of the chocolate glaze from the bottom of the plate, she looks up and smiles. A genuine smile. She has a bit of chocolate on the edge of her mouth.

"You have a little..."

I reach forward, but she swats my hand away and grabs her napkin.

"Don't you dare." Her smile is gone. Her glare is back.

"Just trying to return the favor from this morning."

"No, thank you."

As we walk through the other diners on the way to the exit, without realizing it, my hand goes to the small of her back. She stiffens and steps out of my reach.

Got it. No touching.

Once in the hallway, I point to the stairs down to the first floor. "I have something else planned. This way."

She sighs wearily. "Can we be done?"

Now that I'm starting back at the beginning of softening her toward me, I can't waste any time.

"Only if you want to forfeit," I respond.

Reluctantly, she follows me down the stairs from the third floor to the main floor. This staircase reminds me of the stairwell in the movie *Titanic*, and we all know how that ended. Dinner went well overall, but I'm not feeling optimistic about our bet right now, and I can relate to a sinking ship. Hopefully tonight and tomorrow I make up for the ground I lost.

On the first floor is an enormous Christmas tree, at least fifteen feet high. Guests have already gathered.

"What are they all doing here?" Meg asks. "What are *we* doing here?"

I check the time on my phone. "In ten minutes, they're having a tree lighting ceremony."

She's frowning. I thought this would be fun. Was I wrong?

"But the lights were on last night when I arrived," she says. "Did you bribe them to do it again? Maybe threaten their livelihood?"

Is this another dig at my chosen career? Does she think I

take personal delight in the misfortune of others? It's better to just ignore the comment and pretend this is fun.

"According to the event schedule at the front desk," I say, "They do the tree lighting every night over the week leading up to Christmas. Google says that tree-lighting ceremonies are pretty standard Christmas movie fare. This is fun, right?"

She swivels to look at me. "Do *you* think it's fun? You don't like Christmas."

"I like the *idea* of Christmas. Time off work. Family. Good food. I don't get the *hype* around Christmas," I clarify. "There's a difference."

"Please enlighten me."

"Christmas is an excuse to go into debt to buy people stuff they don't need just to prove you love them."

She shakes her head in disagreement. "You give gifts not to prove love, but to show love."

I scoff. "Maybe you do, but that hasn't been my experience."

"You always give Matt and my parents expensive gifts. Are you saying you do it to prove you love them?"

Essentially, yes. But I can afford it. So many families can't afford the expectations of the holiday.

I move us around to the opposite side of the stairs, where the view is better. The crowd grows. Meg smells nice, something floral, maybe a little fruity. When someone pushes into her side, she leans into me and doesn't seem to realize it since she doesn't move away like I'm a hot stove. Her attention is on the tree, so I don't think I can count that as a win. If she were aware, she'd back away. It's hard to forget the "ew, ew, ew," from this morning when she touched my lip.

The lodge manager takes his place on a raised dais and rings a bell. He's wearing a red coat and a tall, black top hat like he's a circus conductor. Is that normal for a tree lighting? It does add a dramatic flair.

"Welcome to our tree lighting ceremony," the manager says. "It thrills us to have you at Nordquest to celebrate your Christmas holiday."

He talks for a few minutes about Christmas cheer and the activities they offer over the next few days. Before people get restless, he invites a child from the audience to come up with his mom to push a big red button. Hundreds of lights on the tree burst into color and everyone applauds.

It's a little anticlimactic.

"What do you think?" I ask.

Her eyes sparkle and the angst from earlier is gone as she says, "That *was* fun. I've never been to a real tree-lighting ceremony before. The tree is beautiful."

I slump in relief. All is forgiven. "They have refreshments. Cookies and cocoa."

She shakes her head. "I couldn't eat another bite. Come on, it's my turn now. I have the perfect activity."

She takes my elbow and tugs me up the stairs. Once we're on the third floor, she drags me to the end of the hall. When she stops, her smile is as big as the Nile and as deep as the Grand Canyon. There's a glint in her eyes I don't trust.

She removes her heels and hangs them from her fingers, then sighs with relief as she wiggles her toes. "What song should we sing first?"

I look around, wondering if I missed half the conversation. "Song?"

"We're caroling."

I take a few steps back. “No, we’re not. You might like to sing, but I definitely don’t.”

“Are you giving up on our bet already?” She taunts.

I look around the hall again. We’re the only people here. “You’re seriously going to make me carol? Carolers should wear scarves and hats that hide most of their faces and big coats and mittens to make them unidentifiable to their neighbors. It should not be in the middle of a ski lodge hallway.”

“Says who? Are there police who go around and arrest people who don’t abide by the caroling laws?”

I step close and say quietly, “I don’t know if you remember, but not only do I not enjoy singing, I also suck at it. If I sing, guests will complain to the lodge management and get us both kicked out of here.”

“Or they might enjoy our song and appreciate the few minutes they have to listen.”

She honestly doesn’t remember. I took choir the first half of our sophomore year, so we’d have another class together. Every time the tenors practiced a part alone, our teacher grimaced. I didn’t understand why until the kid I stood next to told me I was off-key. From that moment on, I mouthed the words and everyone was happier, especially our teacher. I dropped the class at the end of the semester and haven’t sung since.

“Come on,” I beg. “Can’t you pick something else for us to do?”

“Nope.” She seems to take delight in making me miserable.

I’m not singing. “I’m not sure I know the words to any Christmas songs.”

"What about 'Jingle Bells?'"

"Nope."

"Liar. Sing, or you forfeit." Her eyes brighten with the threat.

Everything becomes clear. She wants me to forfeit. All day, her activities were meant to make me want to give up. She's forgiven nothing.

I'm not easily deterred from tasks I set for myself. I'll prove to her I'm not the idiot from high school, and if I have to sing to do that, so be it.

I can only hope that everyone went down to the tree lighting ceremony and haven't returned so it's only Meg who will suffer.

"I know 'Jingle Bells,'" I say.

She picks a pitch. "Jingle Bells, Jingle Bells. Jingle all the way."

Her voice is beautiful. She was in the premiere show choir in high school. I don't want to ruin her solo, but when she elbows me, I join in. Her grimace lasts a split second, but I caught it. I hope she regrets making me sing.

Then Meg *knocks on a door.* It opens and an older woman stands on the other side. I expect her to throw rotten fruit. Instead, her husband joins her and they watch us and smile. That is a look of enjoyment, not torture. It's a mystery.

After singing Jingle Bells twice, Meg ends the song.

"How lovely," the woman says and they both clap. Their hearing aids must be turned off. "Thank you so much."

"Merry Christmas," Meg says.

"Merry Christmas to you both," her husband chimes in.

We turn away, and I heave a sigh of relief. "That wasn't so bad."

"Good, because we have the whole hallway." She waves at the expanse before us.

"I don't think so," I say. "Once was enough."

"Just say you forfeit and we'll stop now."

I remain silent. Meg knocks on the next door and we sing. Over the next eternity, I lose count of how many people are subjected to our caroling. We cycle through "Frosty the Snowman," "Deck the Halls," and "Jingle Bells." The only songs where I know most of the words.

Not everyone answers the door when Meg knocks. Those who do, show varying degrees of enjoyment. A few I'd classify as annoyed. Some wince, but not as many as I'd expect.

Their response doesn't dim Meg's enthusiasm. She choreographs little dance steps to add to the songs. I'm sure it's meant as more torture for me, but I join in and make sure to look happy doing it. It's so ridiculous it's actually fun.

Meg is fun. I've forgotten how much fun we had in high school. She never liked a lot of attention, unless she was singing on a stage. She's changed over the years. She's more confident and comfortable in her own skin.

When we reach the end of the hallway, I'm finished.

"We're done," I say with finality.

"We have more floors to visit."

"Have fun on your own. I'm going back to the condo." I head toward the elevator.

"Fine. Forfeit," Meg calls out behind me.

I turn back around. "No way. I humiliated myself in front of dozens of people. Whole families are laughing behind closed doors. I did not forfeit."

She rolls her eyes. "Fine. We're done."

She follows me to the elevator. Once back at the condo, we come to an abrupt halt when Matt stands up from the table. He leans against it like he's about to fall over. He looks better, but his expression is sullen.

"Where were you guys?" He turns accusing eyes on Meg. "I thought you decided not to go to Quest."

Her cheeks are pink, but she is unrepentant. "You have nothing to worry about. I'm fine. I'm not stupid anymore."

A silent conversation bounces between them that I can't decipher.

Matt looks from Meg to me, then gives us a decisive nod. "Fine. Your potato soup didn't sit well. Can you get me more water and Pepto?"

"Sure. Let me help you back to bed."

As they walk toward the hall, Matt shoots me a glare. I'm sorry he's sick, but does that mean he expects me to stick around and be miserable as well? When he twisted his ankle in New York and stayed in the hotel for a day, he didn't ask any of us to stay back with him. Why does my hanging out with Meg make him angry?

Chapter Twelve

MEG

I SHOULD FEEL BAD ABOUT HOW SICK MATT IS, BUT MOSTLY I'M resentful that he took trips to Salt Lake every February and never let me know. He's busy at work and with his social life, but when he was so close, why couldn't he ignore Noah and make me a priority for at least one night?

Two days before Christmas is not the time to have this conversation. I'm not sure there will ever be a right time. As upset as I am, I stay silent and help him into bed. It's in my DNA to take care of sick people, even when I'm angry at the patient.

"Did you forget about my warning?" he asks.

"Your warning about not falling for your best friend? No forgetting. I remember."

"You two looked cozy when you came in. You completely forgot about me being sick. You're getting too wrapped up in him. Tomorrow, ignore him. I'll tell him the same thing."

I'm two seconds away from throttling Matt. As if he has any right to tell me what to do. If there was anyone else here and I hadn't made a bet I am still intent on winning, I wouldn't have spent the day with Noah. But I did. *So deal, Matt!*

"We're not kids anymore," I say. "Stop treating me like one."

Matt sinks deeper into the mattress. "I'm your big brother. I only want to protect you. Noah breaks hearts. That's who he is."

I know that from personal experience. But today, Noah just seemed lonely.

"He seems lonely," I say.

The sigh Matt gives me is like someone chewing corn chips with their mouth open.

"Trust me," he says. "Noah is never lonely when he's traveling. I know him better than you."

I lift my hands in surrender. "Believe me when I say I will never forget he's your best friend."

I leave and head down the hall to check in with my parents. Mom's sitting up in bed working on her laptop, her reading glasses perched on her nose. She looks up as I enter.

"You're feeling better?" I ask.

"Better, but weak. I don't think I'll be doing any skiing this trip, but I'm definitely on the mend." She points to dad next to her. He's rolled up in a ball on his side. She shakes her head. "I'm not sure if he's sicker than I am or just more sensitive, but he's still not well."

I smile. "Do you want anything? More soup? Water? Pepto?"

"You're such a sweetie, but I'm fine for now."

"What are you working on?" I ask as I step further into the room.

"Going over a few ideas my assistant sent me for the Valentine's Day Gala we're planning." She pats the bed beside her. "What did you get up to today?"

I sit next to her and lay my head on her shoulder. She runs her fingers through my hair.

"I convinced Noah to go caroling with me along the third floor."

Mom laughs. "What? That kid refuses to sing. How did you convince him?"

I don't want to get into the specifics of our bet, so I say, "It wasn't as hard as you might expect. We also went to the tree lighting downstairs. Oh! And to dinner at Quest. It was delicious."

She groans, half in agony and half in regret. "I want to be jealous, but anything more than potato soup would do me in. Was it as amazing as I've heard?"

"Better."

I would go on and describe every morsel, but in her current situation, I might put her off food for good. Instead, we talk about her New Year's party plans and a few other events she's planning for clients. I miss moments like this. I've been stupid to stay away from my parents for so long. They may love me least, but their least is still a lot.

"Good night," I say.

"Love you, Meg."

When I get back to the kitchen, Noah's leaning against the counter, his arms crossed, as if he's waiting for me.

"What?" I ask.

"You have one more activity."

"Huh?"

"You owe one more activity to reach your five. It's only eight o'clock. What are we going to do?"

I'd really like to climb into bed and watch a movie, but a bet is a bet. For my last activity, I want to walk the town loop and look at the shop windows. Because of their extended holiday hours, everything is open until nine.

The tortuous part for Noah will be the visit we make to the old-fashioned ice cream parlor on the loop. He is not a fan of ice cream, which makes it the perfect activity. I'm still over-full from dinner, but ice cream will fill in the cracks.

"Ice cream in town," I say.

His head falls back and grumbles before capitulating. "Okay."

My phone rings. It's my roommate, Livy. She must have gotten her phone to work since it's her number on the screen and not the stranger she borrowed a phone from last night.

"I'll go change and take this call. Will you get Matt water?"

"Sure."

I answer the phone as I disappear into my room.

"Livy! Your phone works. Have you fallen in love yet?"

"Not even close. I give you an A for enthusiasm, though."

"Tell me everything."

I put the phone on speaker and change into jeans and a sweater while she talks. She's stuck at the inn in Wyoming because the storm is still spitting out snow and the wind is making the roads impossible to drive. So she made sugar cookies, her specialty.

"You've reminded me of that Christmas movie," I say. "About the girl who owns a bakery and gets this huge order for Christmas cookies that she doesn't have time to complete on her own, so she hires help from the temp agency. Do you remember? One of the temps is super-hot with beautiful biceps. Does the nice father who saved you from certain death on the side of the road have nice biceps?"

Against my will, I think of Noah shirtless this morning. He has nice biceps. Nice abs. Even his wrists are attractive.

"I haven't noticed." She's lying. There's that thread of deceit in her voice I've spent years learning how to detect.

"In the movie," I say, "Big Biceps also has nice lips. Have you checked out his lips yet?"

I burst out in giggles, and a second later Livy joins me.

"You're being ridiculous," she says.

"Maybe. But isn't ridiculous a lot more fun than realistic?"

"I better go," she says. "Have you heard from Layla?"

I realize for the first time today that she didn't respond to the text I sent her this morning. I feel like a terrible friend, but I'm not surprised by her silence.

"No," I say. "She'll respond when she's ready."

We say goodbye, and I head out into the living room.

Noah waits by the front door. "Ready?"

I nod, and we head out.

WALKING THE LOOP OF NORDQUEST IS JUST LIKE WALKING through the main street of any small town in any Christmas movie. Snowdrifts separate the plowed road from the shoveled sidewalks. Every shop has colored lights and a holiday display in the window. Even though the temperature is below freezing, people are still outside, greeting each other as they visit the different stores. Everything is friendly and festive.

As we walk, it begins to snow. I look up at the gray sky and the soft flakes floating down. If I were with someone I trusted and respected, this moment would be perfect.

Though, when I think about it, aren't movies all about imagination and the suspension of disbelief? I can use my imagination to pretend I'm in a scene with someone I actually want to spend time with.

Then Noah has to speak and ruin the perfection inside my head.

"Why ice cream in the dead of winter?" he asks. "We're not even inside in front of a fire, but outside where it's already cold."

"You don't mind the cold," I counter. "Every winter, you wore shorts and nothing heavier than a jacket. You claimed you were stronger than the weather."

"Yeah, but I wasn't ingesting ice cream while standing in a snowstorm."

I wave my hand around at the scattered flakes. "I'd hardly call this a storm."

"Ice cream is more appropriate for summer."

"During the summer, a popsicle is a better option than ice cream. Yes, ice cream is cold, but it's too heavy for a hot day. Instead of giving pep like a popsicle, it weighs a person down. Ice cream is perfect for winter. It has sustenance and gets the body working on digestion."

"Popsicles are boring."

We've transported back to high school when we spent lunch squabbling with each other about silly things, like the best Studio Ghibli movie (me: *Howl's Moving Castle*, him: *Spirited Away*), the best candy bar (me: Twix; him: Skittles, which is technically not a candy bar and led to more squabbling), and the best day of the year (me: December twenty-fifth; him: April twenty-fifth, because it's not too cold and it's not too hot. He only said that because it was a quote from my favorite movie).

The memories of our friendship this conversation unearths fills me with sadness. This whole day, Noah has been nice and friendly. Why couldn't this be the real him, and not just a temporary version? Why did he have to ditch me the second he made better friends? The moment Matt feels better, Noah will forget about me again.

I don't want him to forget about me again.

Crap.

He's snuck in through my defenses. When I go back down the mountain in two days, I'll miss him. I'm unprepared for the sense of loss that overwhelms me. It feels like a new hurt, and not one that scabbed over eleven years ago.

"Are you okay?" Noah asks. "Meg, what's wrong?"

"Nothing's wrong. I'm fine." I clear my throat of the emotion clogging my voice and rub the tears from my cheeks. "Just shocked by your ignorance on the topic of cold foods to eat during which season."

"Meg."

I wish he would stop saying my name so tenderly. He has no right to pretend to care.

A bookstore comes up on our right. I need a break from him. If he presses, I may say some of what I'm thinking. I refuse to be the butt of his jokes anymore.

"I'm going in here." I head inside. "I'll meet you out front in ten minutes."

Plenty of time to plug up the holes in the walls protecting me from his influence.

The romance section is at the back, and I head in that direction. There's an eclectic mix of new and used books stacked in precarious piles. It smells old and like fire kindling. I love it. I'd love it more if Noah didn't follow me.

"Meg, seriously, what's wrong?"

"Nothing." I smile.

"You're smiling at me. A clear sign that something's wrong."

"Can I have a few minutes to browse?" Then I tack on, "Please."

He scratches his cheek and studies me. Maybe he needs more explicit instructions.

I point across the small store. "Go wait over there."

I can't keep up eye contact, so I look back at the shelves. I travel along the first row, and Noah follows. This is the Noah I don't like. The one that ignores me, or at least my requests.

"What kind of romance are you interested in reading?" I say conversationally while stewing inside. "If I find you a good one, will you then go to a different part of the bookstore and read it?"

"Did I make you upset by arguing about ice cream?" he asks, ignoring my attempt to get him to leave. "You know I was joking, right? I thought we were having fun, kind of like in high school."

So, he does remember things about our short friendship, and fondly, if I had to judge by the softness in his voice. I wondered. It makes me feel worse.

"I've asked you to leave me alone." There's a sharpness to my tone. I hope he hears it and takes it seriously. All my pent-up frustration with him and Matt is very close to the surface.

I head down the second aisle.

"Can I ask you a question?"

"No," I say. "I'm pretty sure I don't want to answer it."

"You're having fun, right? I know there have been some rough patches today, but overall, I think it's been great to spend time together again. Have I at least improved your opinion of me a little bit?"

I swing around to stare at him. "Are you serious? You think you've done anything to make me like you? You're delusional."

He takes a step back. Then another. The gentleness from minutes before is gone, replaced by flat lips and flared nostrils.

"Why do you despise me? When did you become so unforgiving? Yeah, I screwed up after making the baseball team, but I'm not that person anymore. I gave you the space you asked for. For years. And yet you still can't forgive me for being an idiot sixteen-year-old boy? Are you going to hold this against me for the rest of my life? People change. I've changed. Don't I get to redeem myself?"

What the heck is he talking about?

"Whatever," I say with a head flick.

He closes his eyes and takes a deep breath. "I'm sorry, Meg. I'm sorry. How many more times do I have to apologize before you forgive me?"

This is the first apology I've ever heard, and it irritates me he doesn't acknowledge that fact. Words to that effect pile up inside my head and I don't want to hold them in anymore. We're having this conversation, *now*. But not here. I grab his wrist and head out of the store. Once outside, I pull him between two buildings, out of the way so people won't notice us.

"You never apologized," I say. "You never once tried to talk to me after that kiss. Oh right, except for the text you sent telling me you made the team. Then complete silence."

He huffs while shaking his head. "I put notes in your locker for a full week until Matt said you wanted space. And what about the email I sent you at the beginning of our senior year? I told you how I felt and you ignored my feelings like they were beneath you."

I am completely lost. "Did you ghost another classmate, one of your many admirers perhaps, and confuse the two of us, because I never got any email from you. I never got a note in my locker. I got nothing."

He looks at the ground, his hands on his hips. "Why are you lying? I know you got them. I apologized over and over, and yet you still ignored me."

"I ignored you?" I let out a short scream. A cloud of white billows out of my mouth. "You can't rewrite our history."

"I'm not the one doing that."

I poke him in the chest, as hard as my finger muscle can manage, hoping to inflict pain as I remind him of how things really went down in high school.

"When you made the baseball team and started ignoring me, I understood. Matt told me how I embarrassed you. How you called me clingy. Still, I hoped. I waited for you to remember me. I thought we could at least spend time together outside of school where all your cool friends wouldn't see. Except you never came back. I went to Winter Formal stag with a few of my girlfriends. I had to watch you with your date and know that I wasn't good enough for you anymore."

My voice cracks, but I can't stop talking. Things I've held in for years are all coming out now.

"And yes, high school was a long time ago. It doesn't even matter anymore. I don't care about that stupid kiss or Winter Formal or all the horrible things you said behind my back. I've moved on.

"What I *do* care about is what happened after high school. Matt was supposed to go to college with me here in Utah. We'd planned it for years, but then at the last second, he decided to go to Texas with you. I never applied to Texas. You two left me behind. That was your plan, wasn't it? Get rid of your best friend's annoying sister."

I scrub at my face. I don't want to cry over this, but I can't stop. "You guys go on trips. Come here to ski and don't bother to tell me. You stole my brother. He's *my* twin, and yet for whatever reason, you're the sibling he wishes he had."

Noah stands with his jaw open, his brows furrowed. As if he didn't live through these events.

"And my parents?" I'm yelling now. "You show up in Idaho Falls, and they drop everything to cater to you. They love you more than they love me, and I'm their daughter. They traveled across the country to see you and Matt play multiple times, and yet they struggle to drive three hours to see me in Salt Lake City.

"All I wanted this year was my family to myself without you taking them away. I thought I could rebuild some of my relationship with my brother if you weren't here distracting him. Instead, I'm stuck with *you*."

He's shaking his head, his face white. "I didn't know, Meg. I'm sorry."

"You didn't know? This is all fact. You were there for all of it. And you won't let me watch my Christmas movies. They make me happy. You make me miserable."

Without another word, he turns and walks back the way we came, dodging people as he goes.

"I'm not finished. Noah!"

Chapter Thirteen

NOAH

ANGER BEATS THROUGH MY BODY WITH EVERY STEP. THE EDGES of my vision turn black. My breath is ragged as if I'm running when I just manage to stay upright as I walk back to the lodge.

"Noah!"

I hear Meg's voice, but it doesn't penetrate the furious haze that clouds my thoughts. All I know is that there is one variable that explains the years of misunderstanding between me and Meg.

Matt.

I don't care that he's sick. I have questions, and I need honest answers. If he even knows what the word "honest" means. After everything Meg told me just now, I have my doubts.

I'm back at the condo, having noticed nothing around me

on the return trip. I burst through Matt's bedroom door and flip on the overhead light.

He groans as he rubs his eyes and sits up. "What are you doing? I was asleep."

The rough edge in his voice adds heat to my fury. He's been lying to me for years, and now I should take it easy on him because he ate an undercooked beef taco?

"Throughout high school," I say slowly, fury in every word, "You said Meg needed space. That she was the type of person who takes a long time to forgive. I never talked to her because you said it would annoy her. I wrote notes, and you slipped them into her locker for me. But she never got them, did she? And what about the email I wrote her senior year? You told me she read it, but didn't want to try friendship again. Did you get on her computer and delete the email from her inbox? Why would you lie to me?"

He squints at me. "We're talking about high school?"

Generally, I don't fight. I don't argue. That's how my parents solve disagreements, not me. Until now. I want a brawl.

"Yeah," I say. "We're talking about high school."

"That was nine years ago. Why does this matter now?"

I'd hoped for some plausible explanation for his lying, but he deflects. I ball my fists, but hold steady, even as my muscles quiver with barely contained rage.

"It matters because you *lied*. And the lying never stopped. An hour ago I stood in this room, and you told me to ignore Meg. If I upset her, she might leave and that would disappoint your parents. Is that really the reason you didn't want me to talk to her? Or maybe it was because you didn't want me to find out the lies you've been telling both of us."

All these years I thought he had my back, but he was only covering his own.

"I ..." Matt trails off, and shrugs. "She was holding you back. I did what had to be done. Not just for you, but for all three of us."

I roll my shoulders and try to follow his explanation. It makes no sense to me. "Holding me back from what?"

"A true high school experience. Friends, fun, sports, travel. During your first year in Idaho Falls, you had one friend. Meg. When you made varsity, you were friends with half the school. Meg didn't fit into that world."

What does that even mean? I could have been friends with Meg and half the school. Meg wasn't on another planet.

I scoff. "That's a weak excuse for lying."

Matt lets his patented sigh last as he studies me. "Meg was stuck in her safe, small existence. You and I, we're meant for something bigger. Better. She didn't want the spotlight. She would have hated being the center of attention. Your friendship never would have lasted. You couldn't see that, but I could. I just pushed forward the inevitable outcome."

Yeah, I'm not buying it. "Maybe, but maybe not. That wasn't your call to make."

"Someone had to make it. You're both happier living your own lives."

The garbage coming out of his mouth would be laughable if it wasn't so agonizing. Matt was the one person I thought I could trust. When my injury in college kept me from playing baseball professionally, he made sure I got myself out of bed in the morning and ate more than frosted flakes for every meal. He helped me move my mom into rehab. Twice. He flew out to Washington with me for a week when my dad was in a serious car accident.

His betrayal is unlike anything I've ever known.

"Matt, you know better than anyone how my parents have lied and manipulated me just to get back at each other. And you've done the same thing, except you pitted me against your sister."

"Whoa." He stands as he shakes his head and holds out his hands as if to calm me down. "I am not like your parents."

"Yeah, you are. You had no right to decide Meg and I were better off not being friends."

"You would never have made the decision for yourself."

"That was my choice!" I yell. "You can't tell me you've been lying for eleven years and your only motivation was so I'd have an ideal high school experience."

"Shhhh. You'll bring my parents out here asking questions."

I don't want to upset Calvin and Judy. I guess that means no giving Matt a bloody nose.

I quiet my voice. "Why did you really lie to us?"

He pinches the bridge of his nose as If I'm the one trying his patience. "Meg is ... odd. She doesn't like most people, but if you're one of the few she does like, she holds on with both hands and doesn't let go. Because we're twins, I'm one of those unlucky people she likes. She expected us to do everything together, but you and I are different. Meg and I never shared the same friends or interests, but she wouldn't let me go. When you made the baseball team and stopped talking to her, I saw an opportunity. Whenever we hung out, she avoided us."

And there it is. The other shoe drops. I didn't believe this could get worse.

Slowly, because I don't want this to be true, I say, "You invited me over to your house after practice to keep your sister away?"

"You were excellent pest control." He chuckles weakly like it's funny and I should join in on the joke. He notices my expression because he instantly sobers. "At first. But after a while, you really became my best friend. My parents love you. All those nights after games they'd take us out to dinner, just the four of us. Those were good times."

I collapse onto the edge of his bed, the disappointment and pain overcoming my anger. All of this from the person I trust the most in my life.

"You used me." My voice is strangled, my throat tight.

Matt sits on the bed next to me. "Our friendship was inevitable, with or without Meg in the equation. I didn't use you. I helped you. I helped all three of us. Meg is happy in Salt Lake City. She has friends and a job she loves. If she'd tagged along with us in high school and on to college, she wouldn't have that."

But she'd have me. I would have her.

"Believe me," he continues, "If she'd known we were heading to Texas, she would've made sure to come with us."

I loved my college years, and the only way they could have been better was if Meg was there. Noah has taken so much from me, and he can't see that.

I stand and head to the door. "I can't talk to you. I don't know what to think or how I feel. All I know is I don't trust you anymore."

"Come on, man," Matt says. "Can't we let this go?"

"No."

The door's half closed. I open it fully and find Meg standing against the opposite wall, tears streaming down her face.

"How much did you hear?" I ask her.

"All of it." She wipes her cheeks with the sleeve of her coat.

"I'm sorry." I don't think she'll ever understand how much. If I could protect Meg from the truth of what her brother has done, I would.

"You're not the one who should be apologizing," she says softly.

She pushes against the wall and heads into Matt's room.

I want to stop her. Instead, I move out of her way.

Chapter Fourteen

MEG

Matt rolls his eyes as I enter his room. "What now?"

All this time I've blamed Noah for driving a wedge between me and Matt, but it's been Matt who used Noah as the wedge. I feel itchy in my skin like all this anger and hurt need an outlet before I blow up.

"Why do you hate me?" It's a whisper.

I don't know how to have this conversation, or even if I want to. Whatever comes out of Matt's mouth will hurt more than what I've already heard, and that was excruciating.

He huffs out a breath and shakes his head impatiently. "I don't hate you, Meg. I love you. You're my sister. But as a teenager, I wanted space. You lived a small existence, and you expected me to live the same way. I like people. I love sports. I wanted to go to parties with my friends on the weekends, and you wanted me to stay home and watch movies with you. I wanted my own life."

"I just wanted to spend time with you."

He rolls his eyes. "Is that what it was when you insisted we develop a twin language in fourth grade? Every day for weeks, you forced me to learn the words you made up. It was awful."

I remember, but it's a happy memory, not a tortured one like it is for Matt.

"All our Halloween costumes had to match," he continues. "Frodo and Sam. Woody and Buzz. Mustard and ketchup. It was embarrassing."

I thought it was fun.

"Middle school was worse." He's on a roll now. "You wanted us to sign up for the same classes. We had to eat lunch together. Instead of finding your own friends, you wanted to hang out with mine. We're different, Meg, but you never saw that. I'd had enough. I did us both a favor when I stopped being Tweedledum to your Tweedledee. We finally had our own lives."

Is it terrible to want to spend time with my brother? Is that something I need to feel guilty about? Because this feels like my fault, and I do feel guilty.

"You didn't have to lie to me," I say. "You could have told me the truth."

His nose wrinkles. "No, I couldn't. You were fragile."

I snort at that. "I was never fragile."

"Well, Mom and Dad sure thought so. 'Be careful with Meg. She's not like us.'"

It shouldn't surprise me they'd say something like that, but it does. It makes me feel "other" instead of simply different. In a way, it makes sense. After my visits with the therapist ended, they did treat me like I was fragile.

Matt continues. "If they ever found out that I told you I wanted my own life, they would have freaked. It had to be your choice to keep away from me."

"So, you used Noah." It's a statement. Not a question.

He juts out his jaw. "I didn't *use* him. It was an opportunity for all three of us."

He's stubborn. I don't try to convince him he's been a selfish egomaniac. I don't want to waste my energy.

"And now?" I ask. "We're both adults and have been for some time. We live in different states. You still have to lie? You can't even give me a five-minute phone call?"

He takes a deep breath and sighs as if my question is stupid. "I give you five minutes; you expect my whole weekend."

A spark of anger flares in my chest. "How would you know? You haven't given me five minutes since we turned sixteen. Maybe I expected too much from you growing up, but I'm not that person anymore. You could have told me the truth, and I would have listened. You never gave me a chance. I was a stranger to you then, and I'm a stranger to you now."

Matt shakes his head. "I know you, Meg. You haven't changed at all. I'm sorry the truth hurts."

"You think I'm upset because of your truth?" My voice rises. "If you told me how you felt ten years ago, I would have been hurt by the truth. I'm hurt now because you lied to me for half our lives."

I want to wipe that know-it-all look off his face, but nothing I say will change his mind. He's so sure he's right.

"Meg, I'm exhausted. Just don't tell Mom and Dad, okay? No one likes a tattletale."

That's what he's concerned about. Not the devastation he's caused Noah and me. So be it.

"You get your Christmas wish, Matt. I'll leave you alone. Not just for tonight, but from now on. No more phone calls. No more begging for some of your time when I visit Mom and Dad. You are welcome to pretend I don't exist. Because going forward, I can promise I will do the same."

I leave his room, and there's Noah, waiting in the hallway. He looks at me tenderly and reaches out a hand. I shake my head. I can't process everything right now. Noah is supposed to be the horrible person, not my brother. I need time to think.

Matt calls out just loud enough to be heard in the hallway, "You'll both figure out I did the right thing. I'm not the bad guy."

"That's usually what the bad guys say," Noah mutters.

I step into my room and shut the door. I crumble to my bed and muffle my tears with my pillow. It's a full-body sob as I scream into the feathers.

As I cry, I think through the night's revelations. Tears have a way of clearing my vision and helping me see things clearly.

Matt is like a slot machine. Over the years, he'd give me small wins, enough to make me believe the jackpot was coming, but in the end, I got nothing in return for all my time invested. Our parents see two happy children and have no idea that we don't actually have a relationship. Matt played them as easily as he had me and Noah.

Noah.

The whole situation with Noah cuts deep. I'm not someone who holds grudges. I don't hate people—except for him. Because Matt knew exactly what to tell me so I'd keep my distance. I'm filled with shame over how I've treated Noah over the years, and the whole time he was clueless about why. He must've thought I was a mean, petty person.

The three of us would have gone on indefinitely if not for this week.

I don't care why Matt did what he did. Any reason he gives to explain his behavior is a rationalization to make himself feel better about his lies. What I care about is how his meddling has affected more than my friendship with Noah and my relationship with him.

Weeks ago, after spending an hour gushing to my roommates about Doctor Doug, Layla pointed out that I fall for guys who are unattainable.

"No, I don't," I said at the time. "Why would I do that?"

"Because unrequited love is safer. If they never love you back, you never get hurt."

Her words hit hard because they're true. Doctor Doug is not the only man I've been infatuated with who didn't reciprocate. I've also dated guys who I knew were temporary. That's why I went out with them a second time because there was no potential for the relationship to grow roots.

It all goes back to Noah. Because of that kiss and then nothing. Because I loved him with every part of my fifteen-year-old heart, and he left me without a second thought. It was that easy to leave me.

Or so I thought.

For hours, I stew over the situation. Sleep is evasive. My

eyes are puffy, and my nose runs. I can't seem to stem the tears.

After going through the travel-size package of tissue in my purse, I open my door slowly. The hallway is dark, but for weak lamplight that shines from the living room. It's enough light to see my way to the bathroom to grab a roll of toilet paper. On the way back, I pause.

I owe Noah a long overdue apology. I look longingly at my bedroom door, but decide there's no time like the present.

I step into the living room quietly so I don't wake him if he's fallen asleep. He didn't. He sits on the edge of the couch, fully dressed, coat on. His packed suitcase waits next to him as if he's about to leave. The blankets that make up his bed are still folded on the chair, just like they were this morning.

"You're leaving?" I ask.

He startles at my voice. Maybe it's how congested I sound with all the fluid trapped in my nasal passage, but for a second he looks as if he's just heard a monster. After hours of crying, I probably resemble one.

He glances over for two seconds before looking away. His eyes are red, probably from rubbing them. His hair is wild from running his fingers through the ends.

"I was halfway out the door before I remembered I drove up with your parents," he says. "The bus leaves at eight this morning. I thought I would take it down the mountain."

I step over to the couch and sit on the arm, my feet on the cushion.

I can't say I wasn't thinking of leaving and spending Christmas alone in my apartment just so I wouldn't be around Matt. But I can't leave Mom and Dad. They came here to spend Christmas with me. I won't abandon them.

"Where will you go?" I ask.

"I changed my flight to Baltimore to the twenty-sixth. It's the earliest I could get. I have a hotel in Salt Lake for the next few nights."

There is a certain level of shame in getting exactly what I want but in the worst way possible.

"I realized something tonight," I say slowly. "Matt still sees me as an annoying fourteen-year-old. To him, I've never grown up. I've never changed. He feels justified in treating me like he has because of how I behaved in the past."

I puff out a breath. Apologizing to my sworn enemy at one a.m. is a rough way to start the morning.

"I've done the same to you," I continue. "I'm sorry for not seeing you as a man with the capability to change. You're a good person, and I'm sorry I didn't recognize that sooner."

He doesn't look up from his hands. "You're the one who saw it first, all those years ago, when you invited me to eat lunch with you."

"We had fun, didn't we?"

"Yeah," he nods and gives a short, sad laugh. "We did. Do you know what kills me? We could have avoided all of our misunderstandings if I'd just talked to you myself. Instead, I relied on Matt to be my go-between. He told me to wait it out. To give you time. To not pressure you."

"While he was telling me you had moved on and were mocking me behind my back."

"What a two-faced, selfish jerk." He runs his hands through his hair and tugs on the ends. When he looks up, he meets my gaze. "What you said earlier about your parents loving me more? That's not true. They love you."

"I know."

"Do you? Judy brags about you all the time. Calvin too. They're really proud of you and your work in the hospital. I don't doubt for a second that they would come to you, wherever you were, if you needed them. There is no competition between you and me. You're their daughter. I'm their son's friend."

I appreciate him trying to make me feel better, but he doesn't understand because he's on the inside. He has no idea what it's like being on the outside looking in.

"You're not just Matt's friend to them," I say. "They love you like a son. They'll be devastated if you leave."

He nods. "I don't want to leave, but I can't look at Matt. I can't talk to him. He ... I ... He's not who I thought he was. Without him, I don't feel like I have a place here."

"You'll always have a place in this family."

I want to comfort him and help him bear the pain he must be feeling. The urge to sit next to him and pull him into a hug is strong. I don't. Until a few hours ago, he was my enemy. Now I'm not sure what he is.

"Christmas is ruined for both of us," I say. "We can be miserable alone, or miserable together."

He stills. "What?"

There is no circumstance under which I ever thought I would say these words to Noah. But there was no way for me to predict Matt's betrayal, and here we are.

"Please stay. I'll be sad if you leave."

My words are met with a long silence.

Then, he breathes out, "Okay." He sinks back into the couch.

We sit in silence, both of us unsure of what to do next.

Noah's the first to voice the question aloud. "Where do we go from here?"

"You won the bet. I don't hate you anymore."

He chuckles weakly. "I was supposed to win your good opinion by proving to you I'm a good person. I feel like I cheated by showing you your brother isn't a good person."

"A win's a win. Give me your shoe. You can time me for twenty seconds. Ready?"

This time his smile sticks. "For what it's worth, I enjoyed being stuck in a Christmas movie with you."

Stuck in a Christmas movie. Sounds about right.

"I did, too," I say. "Even if I was using the opportunity to make you miserable. It was fun."

He shakes his head. "I had my suspicions. The worst Christmas movie and an empty cocoa cup? Kids' crafts? Caroling in a resort? Those poor people's ears are probably still bleeding."

I slip down the arm of the couch and sit on a cushion, criss cross applesauce. My knee barely grazes his hip. My heart rate picks up at the mere touch. We both look at the point of contact for many drawn-out seconds.

"Friends?" I ask.

"Friends."

He holds out his hand for a shake. I hesitate for a second, but I can't leave him hanging. That isn't how friends treat each other.

My hand touches his, and I shiver with the contact.

He sandwiches my hand between his two. His fingers are

long and his knuckles large. His skin is soft. My high school best friend isn't sixteen anymore. He's a grown man. He's warm. He's real. I admit to myself I'm attracted to more than just his broad shoulders and tight bum.

I take my hand back and fold my arms across my chest. "We don't have to call a winner to our bet tonight."

"No?"

"Are you up for one more day of Christmas movie magic?"

His eyes widen just enough to show his surprise. "I think I can handle that."

"I'd like to go skiing."

"But you don't like skiing."

I shake my head. "I enjoy skiing. What I don't enjoy is skiing with you and Matt because you leave me behind."

His brow wrinkles. "Matt said you hated it—"

Neither of us continue on with that thought. We both know that anything Matt said is highly suspect.

"So, skiing tomorrow morning?" I ask

"Yeah. That sounds great."

"Then get some sleep."

Before I slip into the hallway, Noah says, "Hey, Meg?"

"Yeah?"

"Thank you."

His words are heartfelt, and I feel my cheeks warm.

"Good night."

I slip into my room, but I don't fall asleep for a long time.

Chapter Fifteen

NOAH

At exactly eight the next morning, Meg bursts into the living room.

"I was thinking," she starts the second she crosses the threshold. "We don't know each other anymore. My parents talk about you, but I don't pay any attention when they do, and anything Matt has told me is probably a lie."

A genuine smile is on her lips, her eyes glow with enthusiasm, and there's a bounce to her step. It's a complete transformation from yesterday. She's neither angry nor miserable. She's alive.

"In so many movies," she continues, "And a lot of books actually, two characters are stuck together and they play games to get to know each other. I thought on the slopes we could try one. What do you think?"

She waits for an answer. I'm still in awe of her, and it

takes a few seconds to catch up on the conversation. "Yeah. That sounds fun."

"Great. How about truth or dare? It's always a popular one."

I grimace.

"No?" she asks.

"I can't stand dares."

Matt can be brutal. I don't think Meg would dare me to do jumping jacks naked in a snowstorm or drink toilet water, but I'd rather not find out.

"Okay," Meg says with a shrug. "Then just truths."

"And if one of us doesn't want to answer the truth?"

"Good point. We'll each get two passes?"

I nod. "Okay."

"I need to check in on my parents and make sure they're set for the day."

I don't want to say the name out loud, but I am curious. "And Matt?"

"Who?" Her expression is completely serious as if I mentioned a stranger.

She disappears down the hall, her ski pants making a swishing noise as she goes.

I grab two protein drinks from the fridge, then turn to see Matt, still wearing his pajamas, in the kitchen. He yawns as he looks me up and down. I'm in my ski gear so it's obvious where I'm headed.

"A ski day?" he says. "I haven't spewed or had diarrhea for almost twenty-four hours. I'm probably fine to hit the slopes, at least for a little while. It's better than hanging out here for another day. Give me ten minutes to change."

"You're not invited," I say.

I'm glad my voice sounds calm, because inside the fury from last night still burns.

"What?" He has the gall to sound surprised.

"Meg and I are going skiing. You're not invited."

He flinches back. "Why are you going skiing with her? Remember what we talked about last night?"

"I remember how you lied to us for eleven years. I'm still waiting for an apology."

Meg walks in. I expect some sort of response from her at seeing Matt, but she breezes by, her smile still in place like he isn't even here.

Matt is going to come to regret the way he's treated Meg, sooner rather than later. She's been a good sister to him, and he will feel the loss. Particularly when he has no one to wait on his every need.

"Ready?" Meg asks.

I hand her the drink. "Yep. How are your parents doing?"

"Much better. Mom thinks they'll head out today. Not to ski, but at least to walk around the town for a bit. They told us to have fun."

Matt huffs. "You can't just ignore me."

Meg does exactly that and walks out the front door.

I'm not as strong-willed as she is. I want him to understand what's going on, and unless someone explains the situation, I'm pretty sure he'll stay ignorant.

I say, "She told you last night you no longer exist to her. Have fun today."

I shut the door behind me.

In the hallway, we run into a few other skiers on their way to the lifts. Meg waves and smiles at them. I've missed this happy, friendly side of her.

We go out the back entrance and head to the ski rental building. Once we have our boots on and our skis and poles in hand, we head toward the slopes.

Fresh snow crunches beneath us. The sun peeks from behind clouds, but the air is cold. The thermostat on the side of the building says twenty-four degrees. It'll warm up as the day goes on, but I doubt it'll get above thirty. It's a perfect day for skiing.

"Do you have a favorite run here?" Meg asks.

Any hurt that might remain from learning about our guys' ski trip is gone. Or maybe just hidden away for now.

"If we go up the Black Bear chairlift, there are a few green runs. I haven't been on any of them, so they'll be new for both of us."

"Okay."

Once we're on the lift, Meg turns in my direction. "First truth. What is your greatest accomplishment?"

I know my answer, but I hesitate. It sounds a bit like bragging.

She knocks her elbow into my side. "Come on. You can tell me."

"My senior year in college, I got the Dick Howser trophy. That's the MVP of the year award for all of college baseball."

Her eyes widen. "Wow. That's amazing. Did my parents fly out for a ceremony? I seem to remember hearing about some award when you graduated."

"Yeah. They were there."

My own parents couldn't make it, but Judy and Calvin came out. It meant a lot to me.

We reach the top and ski down the embankment to the Green Mile Run.

"Ready?" I ask.

Meg doesn't answer, but pulls her ski goggles over her eyes and starts down the hill. I follow. The powder is perfect and offers a smooth ride down the mountain. Matt isn't here, so there is no racing or daredevil tricks. It's just fun. It's over too quickly, and at the end, I have Meg waiting; her goggles are on top of her head so I can see her shining blue eyes.

"That was incredible," she says. "Let's do a more difficult run."

"I'll show you my favorites."

As we ski over to the Elk chairlift, Meg says, "It's your turn. Ask me for a truth."

"Did you volunteer to work Christmas Day to avoid me?"

If I'm responsible for keeping her away from her family, I'd like to know.

She doesn't answer until we're on the lift and on our way up the mountain. "My roommates and I decided to celebrate Christmas together this year. If I was going to be in Salt Lake anyway, I may as well work and let someone else have the day off, right?"

Her cheeks turn pink as she speaks, and it isn't because of the cold.

"What happens when someone lies during the truth game?" I say.

She looks away from the scenery to glance at me. "Are you planning on lying?"

"No, but *you* just did. You could've taken a pass, you know."

She huffs and rolls her eyes. "Fine. I have to take my turn working on Christmas, so I haven't volunteered every year, but this year I did. And yes, I was avoiding you. Do you feel better?"

"Not at all." I definitely feel worse knowing the truth, but it is nice she wanted to spare my feelings. "I would've stayed away from your family Christmas if you'd asked me to."

She looks out across the valley, unwilling to look in my direction. "This is a really slow lift, don't you think?"

When we reach the top, she doesn't wait but leaves me behind. I've raced Matt for years, and this time I don't hold back. I'm at the bottom of the run waiting for her.

I mean to apologize for forcing a confession out of her, but she doesn't give me the chance.

"I'm sorry for lying just now. I'm sorry for avoiding you for years. I wish I could go back and change things, but that isn't possible. Now it's my turn. Tell me the truth about why you don't sing anymore."

I'm surprised by the question. Isn't it obvious? "Because I sound awful. I don't enjoy it. I like to spare the ears of any unsuspecting listeners. Take your pick."

She shakes her head. "You don't sound awful. Trust me. And you loved singing in the sophomore choir until you dropped out. You'd get into the music by bobbing your head or tapping your leg. You left that class every day smiling."

"No, I didn't."

"Cross my heart." She runs her finger across her chest in an X.

"I don't remember."

"I do."

And so our afternoon goes. We go back and forth asking truths all morning, but we stay away from asking anything serious.

I discover Meg finds it impossible to suck on hard candy, which is how she chipped a tooth. She doesn't like horror movies, and can't even watch *Beetlejuice* without having nightmares. Halloween is her second favorite holiday. I had to ask a follow-up question about that, because if she dislikes horror, why Halloween?

"I enjoy handing out candy to the cute kids," she says. "I like eating the leftover candy. I especially love dressing up in fun costumes. This year I was an avocado. My favorite vegetable."

"I'm pretty sure avocado is a fruit. It has a pit."

"No. I would never put avocado in a fruit salad."

"That's how you define a fruit? 'Foods Meg puts in a fruit salad?'"

She laughs. "Yep. Look it up. It's all over Google. I'm surprised you haven't noticed, since you look up everything. I'm pretty sure you're an honorary Google Search Pro."

Somewhere between runs, the game turns to, Would You Rather?

"Would you rather," I say, "Only be able to watch your favorite Christmas movie for the rest of your life, or watch many Christmas movies, but they're all terrible?"

She scrunches up her face and purses her lips as she thinks. It's such a Meg look. I've missed seeing it. "That's a horrible choice to make."

"That's the game," I say with a shrug. "It's supposed to be a hard choice."

"Fine. I would rather watch many movies—"

"Terrible," I interject.

"Many *terrible* movies rather than just one for the rest of my life."

"You're hardcore."

"My definition of terrible is different from yours, and we're going by your definition. Would you rather ..." Meg pauses and studies me with narrowed eyes. "Have silver tinsel as hair, or fingernails that light up like Christmas lights every time you use your fingers."

"For the rest of my life, or just one day?"

"For. The. Rest. Of. Your. Life." With each word, she leans a little closer. She takes this game very seriously.

"You said my question was horrible?" I say with a laugh. "You're brutal. I'll take the tinsel hair. At least then I can shave it off."

Early afternoon we leave our ski gear and head into town for lunch. As we walk, Meg takes long strides and does a partial squat with each step. I watch from behind. She looks absolutely ridiculous, but it's kind of sexy. The movement pulls her pants tight and accentuates her curves. Still, I can't help but snicker.

"Are you laughing at me?" she asks.

"No, of course not. But can I ask what you're doing?"

"I'm stretching. I'm going to be sore tomorrow."

"That's a stretch? Looks more like the mating dance of a bird of paradise."

She stands up straight and walks normally. "Shut up."

"Don't stop on my account. By all means, use this time to stretch." I glance up at the sky and turn in a circle. "You never know. You may attract the attention of a viable mate."

She turns and backhands my biceps, then quickens her step to walk further ahead. I shorten my stride to let her get away. She's trying to hide her laughter, but I can hear it, even from back here.

Chapter Sixteen

MEG

THE SANDWICH PLACE IS PACKED, BUT NOAH AND I DON'T MIND the wait. He goes to order. I stand along the wall until a group leaves their table and I snag it.

While I wait for Noah, I send Livy a text.

Meg: *Any developments with your Leading Man?*

Livy: *We sat up late last night drinking hot cocoa and talking about life.*

As much as I've teased her about her rescuer, I didn't actually think it would go anywhere. Her story is straight out of a movie. What's the likelihood of that happening in real life? Zilch. In her case, I am thrilled that it has.

We text back and forth for a few minutes. She really likes him, and he seems to like her, but she doubts herself.

Livy: *What if, like every other guy I've liked, he decides he just wants to be friends? It would be safer for my heart if I didn't find out.*

The word "friends" sends a pang through my heart. Noah is my *friend.* Such a bizarre, unusual, surprising development.

Meg: *You never win anything when you set out to lose.*

Not exactly true. My bet with Noah? The only way to win is to lose. I've already lost. I don't want Noah to avoid my family for the next two years. I maybe, possibly, even want to kiss him. Just once. It definitely sounds better than licking his shoe. And believe me, two nights ago I would have picked the shoe, one hundred percent.

Livy: *How is Christmas with the fam?*

I'm not sure what to say. Horrible? Surprising? Wonderful? Where do I start?

Meg: *My brother invited Noah to stay with us at the condo.*

Livy: *Your nemesis Noah?*

I glance up and see him heading in my direction with our tray of food. Being with him is effortless. As if no time has passed at all since we were friends in high school. It's confusing, wonderful, and exciting, all wrapped up in one crazy emotion.

Meg: *Yep. He's always been skilled at knowing how to get under my skin.*

Livy: *This sounds like the makings of a Hallmark movie...*

If she only knew. I send an emoji with its tongue sticking out and close the conversation before Noah can see anything on my screen.

"Who are you talking to?" Noah asks as he sits beside me.

"My roommate, Livy."

He moves his chair close, much closer than he needs to. Yes, it's loud with the crowds stuffed in here, but we can still hear each other over the noise of the other diners.

He hands me my bacon avocado (a protein and a *vegetable*!) on sourdough with a side of fries and a handful of fry sauce packets. For my benefit, he wrinkles his nose as he gives me the fry sauce. He is a ketchup man through and through. Silly, really. Fry sauce is ketchup mixed with mayonnaise. Practically the same thing, but better. He doesn't listen to reason. He thinks it's disgusting.

"Where are your roommates?" he asks. "You said earlier you originally planned to spend Christmas with them."

"Livy's in Wyoming. She went to visit her sister. Layla is in Maine with her *fiancé*. She isn't answering any of my texts. It's aggravating."

"Are you worried?"

I dip a fry in fry sauce and swing it close to his face before I place it in my mouth. He wrinkles his nose at the smell. It's ridiculous how he turns up his nose at something so good!

"Yes, but no," I say. "She's a private person and sometimes she has to mull things over before she shares. She'll text us when she's ready. If there was something seriously wrong, she'd let us know instantly. Her silence makes me think things are going okay. Surprising, considering the huge mistake she's made in agreeing to marry *Spencer*."

Noah laughs.

"What?" I ask.

"Just the way you say his name. I feel a kinship. It isn't easy being on your bad side. I pity the man."

He's joking about eleven years of misunderstanding. If he can do that, then maybe I can too. Eventually.

For now, his smile takes a chunk out of my resentment

toward Matt. It's a small piece, but the solid stone of anger in my chest feels lighter.

"There's something I've been wanting to know," I say. "For years, actually."

"Yeah?"

"Why didn't you go into the major league? That's what you wanted, and you were good. You won that trophy, right? So why did you give it up?"

He drops his burger on the wrapper and leans his elbows on the table. "It wasn't by choice. I was in a car accident the summer between my junior and senior year of college."

My blood turns icy. "You were okay?"

He shakes his head. "My prognosis was dicey there for a few months. They weren't sure if I would live."

My heart drops into my stomach. I think my mom mentioned he was in an accident years ago, but nothing life threatening.

"You almost died?" I ask. "How did I not hear about this?"

He smiles. "Just kidding."

I punch his arm. "That was mean."

"It was kind of funny."

When I'm breathing normally again, I ask, "What happened?"

"I broke my wrist." He holds up his right hand. A brace is around his wrist. I noticed it earlier when we left the condo but didn't think anything of it at the time. "And a few ribs. Had a concussion. I sat out of ball practice for a few months. When I came back, I thought I was good to go, but no. My wrist was never the same. The break damaged the cartilage. I have arthritis in the joint now."

I look at his wrist where it lies on the table. "Does it hurt?"

"I try not to use it too much. I have pain meds and the brace when I need it. The cold weather doesn't help. Someday, I may have the bones fused."

He talks about his accident nonchalantly, but I can't believe he really feels that way. He should be playing. He loves baseball.

"There was nothing they could do so you could keep playing?" I ask.

He chews on a fry. "Cortisone shots every two months helped, but there are long-term side effects to cortisone. Nerve damage or the bone can die. I knew I couldn't keep that up for years on end. I throw and pitch with my right hand, and I'm not pro-level with my left. I finished out my senior year, but didn't go any further."

I study his expression and read none of the regret I would expect him to feel.

"You're very stoic about the whole thing," I say. "It must've been devastating."

He leans back in his chair. "Yeah, it was. I wanted nothing else but baseball. But life goes on. I graduated with a business degree and got a job. I came to terms with the trajectory of my life."

I take a bite of my sandwich and wish I could have been there for him. At the time, I didn't care. I can't believe I ever felt that apathetic toward anyone, but especially my former friend.

"Would you rather," I say, "Play major league baseball for thirty years and win all the awards and acclaim and make millions of dollars, but never find love? Or, be married for fifty years and raise a dozen children but never be able to play again? You can't even pick up a bat. Or a ball. Or a mitt."

He whistles. "Brutal choice." He chews on a fry as he thinks. "Twelve kids? That's a lot."

"Well, you're not playing baseball. What else are you going to do?"

He snickers. "I can't do both?"

"No. You have to pick. Baseball, or love."

"Love," he says without hesitation.

"You're sure? Even with *twelve* kids?"

"Positive." He chews another fry. "Besides, you never said I couldn't *watch* baseball."

"You can't watch—"

He holds up his hand. "Too late. I've already made my decision. No changing the terms."

"Fine, new question. If you couldn't have anything to do with baseball, even watching it, would you still choose a wife and a dozen kids?"

He looks intensely at me for a long few seconds. "Mmm ... I guess it would depend on the wife."

When he looks away to eat another fry, I fan my hot cheeks surreptitiously. Lucky hypothetical wife.

THE REST OF THE AFTERNOON IS OUR MOVIE MONTAGE. IF OUR story were on the Hallmark channel, music would play in the background while on screen, viewers watched Noah and I laugh and talk as we ski. I take lots of pictures with my phone. He hams it up, making crazy faces. It's quite difficult, in fact, to get a picture of him smiling normally.

We continue with our games, and I learn all about his life, his stagnant relationship with his parents, the things he loves about his job, and those he doesn't.

One topic we don't broach is Matt. He's a buzzkill, and I want nothing to kill this happy buzz Noah and I have going on.

After dark, we drop our ski equipment off at the rental hut. On the way back to the lodge, we stop in a field next to the parking lot and make snow angels, then an army of mini snowmen. Noah can't resist lobbing a few snowballs in my direction, but instead of having a snowball fight with each other, we decimate our snowmen battalion.

By the time we enter the lobby, my fingers are numb, and my feet are cold. I'm hungry and I'm tired, but I can't remember a time in recent memory when I've felt this happy.

Noah can compete against any one of the leading men in any movie and come out on top. He's funny and gorgeous, considerate and sweet. I have a hundred pictures from today to prove it. Being stuck in a Christmas movie is even better than I could have imagined.

Except if this were a movie showing on television, we would disappoint our viewers.

This isn't a love story. On Christmas Eve I'm heading home. Two days later, Noah flies to Baltimore.

This is a friendship story. After years apart, Noah and I have found our way back to each other.

I make a big production of unblocking his number in my phone.

We promise not to lose contact.

Next time he has a break from work, he'll visit me for a few days.

We have plans for the future. Just not those of the romantic variety. Even if a tiny, itty-bitty, microscopic part of my heart wishes that was a possibility. The rest of my heart is wiser and knows friendship is safe. I appreciate safe.

Chapter Seventeen

MEG

When we arrive back at the condo, Mom's in the kitchen standing at the stove, while Dad and Matt sit on the couch watching what looks like college basketball.

"You're back," Mom says. "Did you have fun?"

"So much fun." I lean in over her shoulder. It looks like she's made chicken chili and smells delicious. My stomach growls.

Mom places her cheek against mine. "You're cold. Soups almost done. Do you want to set the table?"

"Actually," Noah says before I can answer, "I was thinking of taking Meg to dinner at a restaurant in town if that's okay." He turns to me. "Meg? Do you want to go?"

I want to go. I'm not ready to face Matt or deal with the fallout of last night. But should I leave with him? This is a family holiday, and we've hardly spent any time together.

My wish to not have my day with Noah come to an end wins out.

"Mom, do you mind if we don't stay for dinner?"

She shakes her head. "Of course not. We'll have all day together tomorrow. Matt will take any excuse to get out of this condo."

No! I want to avoid him, not spend time with him.

Noah must feel the same because he says, "Oh, I'm sure Matt would rather eat here with you. Greasy food will probably make him feel queasy after what he's been through the last few days."

Mom shakes her head and gives Noah her indulgent smile. "Even if he eats nothing, he needs to go. He's bored out of his mind. It's too bad he felt too sick to go skiing with you today."

Is that what Matt told our parents? Because I heard Noah tell him clearly this morning he wasn't invited.

Unless we want to "tattletale" on Matt the night before Christmas Eve, we're stuck with him. Maybe he'll decide not to come on his own.

"Meg," Mom says, "You use the shower in the master suite. Noah can use the hall bathroom. Go on, get ready for your dinner."

Once showered and back in my room, I take the time to curl my hair and make sure my makeup is perfect. This isn't a date, it's an activity. It isn't unusual to want to look good for dinner with a friend and a conniving brother. (Even if that tiny, itty-bitty, microscopic part of my heart wishes this were a date and my conniving brother was out of the equation).

I grab my nicest pair of jeans, the ones that are most flattering to my figure, and my ugly T-shirt from yesterday. If

Noah can wear his ugly T-shirt to Quest, I can wear mine to a local restaurant. I slip it over my head and glance in the mirror. And burst out laughing.

The idea behind the shirt is still sound. With my shoulders shaking, the garland arms and legs wiggle like the Grinch is dancing. The problem lies with where his hands are placed above his head.

They are exactly over my boobs.

The harder I laugh, the wilder the Grinch dances. It's a vicious cycle that I'm unable to break.

I have to show this to my roommates. Maybe I'll make two more, so we'll have matching shirts to wear around our apartment. They're perfect for the next time we stay in for a movie night.

A knock comes at my door.

"Meg?"

It's Mom. This shirt is too awful not to share, and I open the door.

"Noah and Matt are waiting for you," she says. "What's so funny?"

I take a step back. Her eyes widen, and she covers her mouth as her laughter joins with mine.

"Where did you get that shirt?" she asks.

"I made it!" I say through peals of laughter. "But not on purpose."

Noah shows up behind Mom's shoulder. His jaw drops open, but he doesn't look away. I pull Mom into the room before shutting the door in his face. Me in this shirt is not a visual he should have in his brain.

"I'll be ready in five minutes," I yell through the door, while I still giggle.

"What is with you two today?" Mom asks.

I head to my suitcase to grab something else to wear. "Me and Noah?"

"You two haven't gotten along since high school. I know it hurt you when he took someone else to Winter Formal. I wasn't sure you'd ever forgive him, but yesterday you went to Quest and now you come back from skiing like you're best friends. I think Matt feels left out."

My hands stop rummaging through my clothes. There's so much to unpack from those few sentences. How do I answer? I won't keep what Matt did a secret, and I don't care if that makes me a tattletale, but when we only have one more day together? I'd like us to be a happy family for that one day, even if it's just for Mom and Dad's benefit.

For now, I say the bare minimum. "Noah and I have had some disagreements and misunderstandings in the past, but in the last few days, we've worked through them. Now we're friends again."

It makes me indescribably happy to say that out loud. Noah and I are friends.

She pulls my hair over my shoulders and smooths it down my back. "I don't want to see you get hurt again, so be careful."

I turn to face her. "What do you mean?"

She shrugs, a sad smile on her face. "You were depressed for a long time after your friendship ended. I don't want to see you get tangled up with him once more, only to be hurt when he doesn't stick around."

Me either, Mom. "We're just friends. He travels for work. I know that."

"Good. Now hurry and change. The boys are waiting."

She leaves, and I pull on a teal sweater Layla knit for me last year. Not as entertaining as my Grinch shirt, but appropriate for public display.

Noah's waiting for me right outside my bedroom door. He has on dark slacks and a green button-up shirt. His hair is still damp, and his cologne is just right. Would it be awkward if I leaned in and smelled him?

Yeah, probably.

His eyebrows raise when he sees I changed my top. His lips twitch like he wants to smile but knows he shouldn't. Smart man.

"You will forget you ever saw me wearing that thing," I say with absolute seriousness.

"What thing?"

"Exactly. Let's keep it that way."

We grab our coats, and with a wave to Mom and Dad, we head out.

Unfortunately, Matt follows. Both of us ignore him.

"Truth," I say to Noah. "If you could wish for anything, what would it be?"

With a shake of his head, he says, "Pass."

"What? That's an easy truth."

"My greatest wish is on the tree, and if I tell you, it won't come true. This is one wish I want to come true."

I roll my eyes, even as I find his answer charming. "Fine."

The temperature outside has dropped. Noah, in true movie fashion, doesn't zip up his coat. He does put on a beanie. Not everyone can pull off the beanie look, but he can. He should wear one all year long.

For the entire walk to the bar, Matt says nothing. He trails behind, and we pretend he isn't there. I wish I could take delight in how our roles have reversed, but I can't enjoy it. I've been where Matt is, and it sucks. I'm still angry and hurt by what he did, so I pretend he's a stranger stalking us and push any empathy I feel out the rear window. He doesn't deserve it.

The restaurant is crowded. Every table is taken, and every seat at the bar filled. A live band plays on a narrow platform upfront. It's loud and lively.

Noah turns to me and yells over the noise, "Is this okay?"

"This is awesome."

Apparently earlier today when I wasn't watching, Noah made a reservation, so we only have to wait five minutes to be seated at a table for two near the back. The hostess grabs an extra chair for Matt. It's a tight fit at the small table.

As we peruse the menu and order drinks, the band plays country covers and a Christmas song. After we order, they start into "American Kids" by Kenny Chesney. It has such a good beat; I can't sit still. My knees bounce, and my fingers tap the table. The smile on my face is huge. The ambiance is perfect for a night out with a friend and an idiot brother.

"You want to dance?" Noah asks, even as he looks at me as if he expects to be turned down.

"You know how to two-step?"

"Learned in college. The girls went wild over a guy who knew how to dance. You?"

I'm not a fan of imagining him with other girls, but jealousy is not an emotion a friend feels toward another friend.

I stand and take his hand. "Thursday nights, the university hosted a country dance. I was there every week."

Not only has Noah learned the quick, quick, slow, slow

rhythm of the two-step, but he's also mastered the art of leading. As we move around the dance floor for the next two songs, he twirls me, dips me, does the corkscrew, and even knows the pretzel. I cannot stop smiling. If I'd known Noah could dance like this, I would have overlooked anything and everything I'd thought he'd said about me a long time ago and taken him dancing.

"Suds in the Bucket" ends, and the band begins Tim McGraw's "My Best Friend." It's a slow song. Noah's left hand takes my right. His other goes to my lower back, and he pulls me close.

"Is this okay?" he asks close to my ear.

This is better than okay. "Yeah."

"You know, if I had known there was a live band tonight, I wouldn't have brought you."

I lean back so I can look up at him. "Why?"

"Because your whole family thinks you hate loud music and being around crowds of people."

My stomach drops. "Really?"

"In high school, Matt told your parents multiple times that you refused to go to parties or concerts he invited you to for those two reasons. We all believed him. He's said it many times since. I had no reason to question what he told me, but why do your parents believe Matt when he says stuff like that? It obviously isn't true."

The easy answer is to say my parents just don't understand me. They never have. We're too different.

The long answer isn't so simple.

"My whole family is loud and social," I say. "You've been to enough family parties to know. My aunts, uncles, and grandparents. I'm the exception. When I was a kid and we'd all get together, the noise and amount of people were overwhelming. There would be ten conversations going on in surround sound, and at eighty decibels. Add in the stereo, the clinking of wine glasses and silverware against plates, and it was too much for me. I didn't know how to handle it and threw temper tantrums. By the time I was in middle school, I wasn't as sensitive to noise anymore, but my parents still see me that way."

"Why don't you tell them the truth?"

"I tried. They don't listen."

I'd like to stay in Noah's arms forever. Dancing is an appropriate place for friends to hold each other. Unfortunately, four minutes feels like thirty seconds. The song comes to a close. I think we can squeeze in at least one more dance before dinner arrives.

The band has a different idea.

"Thanks for having us here tonight," the singer says. "We'll be back in twenty minutes."

Applause fills the restaurant, and we join in until the band leaves the platform and takes a table near the front.

Noah slips his hand in mine and leads me to the side and down the hallway to the bathroom where he stops. Before I can ask what he's doing, he speaks.

"Why do you think your parents won't listen? They love you. They want you to be happy, and if they can do something to make you happy, they will do it."

There's a level of fervency in his voice that makes me think my situation is personal to him.

"Why is this so important to you?" I ask.

A group of giggling women walk by to the bathroom. We wait for them to pass, neither of us breaking eye contact.

When Noah answers, his voice is soft, and I have to lean closer to hear.

"I would do anything to have parents like yours. Parents who care. A place to come home to for the holidays. You have that, and you avoid them. They're chasing after you, and you don't care. Do you know how many times they've told me how disappointed they are that you can't make it home? You blame it on your work schedule, but I have to wonder if that's true."

A sneak attack? I wasn't expecting this at all.

"I was avoiding you," I say.

He shakes his head. "Not this summer. I didn't visit once, but neither did you. Truth, Meg, why do you avoid talking to your parents? The person you've been with me the last few days is not the person they think you are."

"Because," I hiss. "I tried. For years. I'm an introvert. They're extroverts. Everyone they know is an extrovert. They'd look at Matt, who is lost without people, and then me, who is lost surrounded by them. Obviously, something was wrong with me. They were worried. They hovered. Then they sent me to a therapist when I was twelve to help with my 'depression.'"

The gaggle of women comes out of the bathroom, and I pause. I can't look up at Noah. This makes it sound like I had a horrible childhood when I didn't. I felt loved, and I was happy, but I also felt misunderstood and like an outsider in my own family. The feeling grew as I entered high school.

Noah hasn't let go of my hand, and once the hallway is clear again, he squeezes it to encourage me to continue.

"I really liked my therapist," I say. "Nancy could see I wasn't depressed. She talked to my parents about my comfort level, likes and dislikes, and they listened to her. They stopped hovering and weren't as worried about me. As I grew older, I changed. But to them, I'm still that twelve-year-old girl. It didn't matter what I said, they referred back to what Nancy told them. It was easier to just let them believe what they wanted and move to Utah."

"That was a long time ago," Noah says. "Try again."

He's so close, I lean my head against his broad chest. He makes me wonder if it is possible they'll listen to me and understand. In the past, I felt like it was a wasted effort.

A loud female voice behind me says, "You two are under the mistletoe."

I turn my head and see an older couple, probably in their seventies, standing beside us. The gray-haired woman points toward the ceiling, and I look up.

What kind of place hangs mistletoe in the hallway to the bathroom? Is this "make-out point" or something?

"Kiss!" The woman says.

She is straight out of a movie, and I laugh. I couldn't have planned it better if I wrote the script and hired an actress to play her part.

I look at Noah. He shrugs. I do owe him a kiss for losing our bet, but I don't want it to be in a bar in front of someone's grandparents. This sort of situation is always so fun to watch in movies but in real life? Awkward.

"Well," the man says when we don't move. "Are you going to kiss this pretty lady, or do I have to?"

Please no.

I nudge Noah with my elbow and tap my cheek. "We can't ignore a Christmas tradition."

Noah, like a gentleman, obliges and kisses me on the

cheek. His lips linger longer than might be appropriate for a friendly kiss, and my heart hiccups at the contact.

The couple clap and then leave us to take care of their business further down the hallway.

"Come on," I say. I don't want to talk about my relationship with my parents anymore. "Our food is getting cold."

When we get back to the table, Matt's nachos are half eaten, but he's not there. I glance around. He's at the bar talking to two beautiful women. He nods when he sees us, which I take to mean he's been watching our food while we've been gone.

We sit and eat, but I can't stop looking at Matt.

"Truth," I say. "If I wasn't here, would you be over there flirting with those girls?"

Noah swallows his bite of hamburger before answering. "Yes, but I'd much rather be here with you. No contest." He knocks his knee against mine under the table. "Truth. If I wasn't here, would you be flirting with that guy over there?"

He nods his head toward the bar where a man sits alone drinking a beer. His glance keeps sliding down to one of the women Matt's talking to. He wears a cowboy hat, Wranglers, a red plaid shirt, and a brown leather jacket. He reminds me of a young Wolverine. I'm a huge Hugh Jackman fan, so I find him attractive, but he's a stranger. I would never approach a stranger in a bar.

"Pass," I say to Noah.

"What?" He laughs. "That's an easy truth."

"So you say." I lean closer to him. "I don't want to make you feel bad about my answer."

He studies me, his eyes tender. "Whatever."

Chapter Eighteen

MEG

THE BAND PLAYS ANOTHER SET. NOAH AND I DANCE TO EVERY song. Slow and fast. If this were a date, it would be the best one I've ever been on. But since it's me with a friend, it's even better. I don't have to worry if he likes me or if he'll ask me out again. We'll continue on like this, and every dinner we share as friends in the future will be just as great.

We don't leave until the band is wrapping up. Matt has already disappeared. With one of those women, or solo, I don't know, and I don't care.

After the heat of the bar, outside is freezing. The temperature has to be in the single digits. In minutes, my face freezes. I zip my coat to the top and wish I'd brought a scarf. Noah takes his beanie from his pocket and puts it on my head.

"You'll ruin my hair!"

He ignores my outcry and pulls it down further so it covers my ears.

"Are you trying to impress someone?" he asks.

"Definitely not you."

The shops are closed, and the sidewalk is empty but for us. Up ahead, a sleigh is on the road pulled by a white horse. The driver is an older man with a white beard, a red coat, and black jeans.

"Is that Santa Claus?" Noah whispers.

"It has to be."

"Should we ask for a ride?"

"It would be criminal not to."

Noah steps to the edge of the sidewalk and flags Santa down.

"Can we get a ride?" Noah asks.

"I was just heading home. It'll cost you extra."

Noah doesn't even hesitate. "Sure. Do you take Venmo?"

"Sure do."

One minute later, we're in the back of the sleigh with a heavy blanket over our laps. Santa pulls back into the road.

If I thought it was cold before, it's nothing like being pulled in a sleigh with the wind blowing past. Even Noah zips his coat up to his chin before draping his arm over my shoulders. I lean into his side. For warmth only. Not because I enjoy laying my head on his chest.

The town is beautiful. White, bright, and peaceful. The cloudy sky reflects the town lights, and it feels too bright for it to be past eleven.

I take pictures of us in the sleigh, the back of Santa's head, the town lights, and softly falling snow. Then I put my phone away and enjoy the ride. It isn't long before the day's activities catch up with me. Between a sleepless night, skiing, and dancing, my limbs are exhausted. My brain is ready for a deep winter's sleep. But not right now. This moment is perfect.

I sink further into Noah. The only sounds are the clomp of the horse's hooves, the swish of the sleigh, and our breathing.

It takes about twenty minutes to do the loop. As we approach the point where we started, Noah calls out, "One more time around? And can you drop us off at the ski lodge?"

"It's late. A twenty percent increase in price."

Santa is quite avaricious, but Noah agrees. I'm not sure how I'll make this up to him. He's spent a lot of money on me the last two days. If he were still my enemy, I might not care, but he's my friend so now I do.

It's another half hour before Santa drops us off at the entrance to the ski resort. I'm glad I don't have to walk far. I'm not sure my legs could carry me further than the sixth floor, and that's with taking the elevator.

Once we're back in the condo, we stand in the kitchen, neither of us moving toward our respective beds. I don't want this day to end. It seems neither does Noah.

And, well, there's the bet. I've thought of little else over the last hour. I don't make it a habit of kissing guy friends, but I am someone who always pays their debts.

"You won," I say. "You should collect your winnings tonight because though our bet technically ends tomorrow, we both know I lost, and tomorrow we'll be with my family all day."

"You want to lick my shoe in privacy?" His grin clues me

in that he's teasing.

"I've seen where that shoe's been today. Did you notice the dirt on the bar floor? I'll take your lips instead."

He runs his hands over his face. "You're sure?"

"I'm sure." I pull my phone out of my pocket and set the timer. "For twenty seconds. I won't cheat you out of your prize."

He hasn't moved, and I'm struck with the fear that maybe he doesn't want to kiss me. Maybe he never did, and was joking about the kiss. Before I can decide how to proceed, he lifts me as easily as if I'm a bag of flour and sets me on the counter.

"That's better."

"What was that for?" I screech. "I'm not a child."

"No, you are definitely not." He glances over my shoulder at the dark hallway. "Shhh, unless you want to wake your family."

I want to be riled up about him lifting me without permission, but he's so close now. His hands are still on my hips, and his face is inches away. He's right. This is much better.

"We're doing this?" I ask. There's a slight quiver in my voice.

"We're doing this."

But then he does nothing. He stands near enough for his breath to caress my cheeks. His eyes scan over my face slowly until they pause on my lips. When I run the tip of my tongue over my bottom lip, his breath hitches. Still, he doesn't move closer.

"Noah," I whisper. "You're torturing me."

"I'm torturing you? I think you have that backward." His

eyes meet mine. "According to the terms of our bet, you're supposed to kiss *me*. I don't—"

I grab his collar and pull him closer. The moment our lips touch, it's like I was holding my breath for the last twenty-four hours, and now I can finally breathe.

Noah's lips move against mine with care and gentleness, but there's a distance in his touch. Like he's counting up to twenty in his head. I don't want him focusing on anything but me.

My arms wrap around the back of his neck, and I pull him closer so he stands between my knees. I deepen the kiss. It takes seconds for his resolve to disintegrate under my onslaught, and he's right here with me, matching me kiss for kiss.

His arms snake around my back. They're large and warm. I feel enveloped by him. Safe. His lips are gentle but hungry. Like he's been waiting for this kiss all day, just like I have. His five o'clock shadow tickles and prickles, a sensation I quite enjoy and a juxtaposition to the softness of his lips. Every part of this kiss is perfect. He's perfect. Best bet ever. Best kiss ever. I never expected losing to be this awesome.

Neither of us are counting seconds now.

I pull away, breathless, but so alive.

"I think that was twenty seconds," he says.

Probably closer to twenty seconds multiplied by fifteen. I could go for another round.

His hands run down my sides to my hips, then to the counter on either side of me. I lean in and press my lips to his neck. His Adam's apple bobs as he swallows.

"I think the original bet was actually for twenty kisses,"

I say.

He laughs wearily and groans as he lays his head on my shoulder. "Meg, it's late. We should go to bed now, or I might never stop."

I turn my head to kiss his chin. "That doesn't sound so bad."

His lips find my temple. Move to the spot next to my ear. My jaw.

"Meg, what are we doing?"

"Kissing. Obviously."

His lips come back to mine, and I sink into the kiss. I have no coherent thoughts. All my focus is on the feel of his hands on my hips, my back, in my hair. The taunt play of his chest muscles beneath my palms.

He abruptly breaks away. I'm cold where his body no longer presses against mine. When I open my eyes, he's five feet in front of me. He rubs the back of his neck and doesn't look at me. The connection between us goes from comfortable to awkward fast.

"We're friends," he says slowly. "Right?"

Oh, yeah. *Friends*. And not the kind that comes with benefits. This was a bet. Nothing more. And why can't it be anything more? Oh, right. Because friendship is safe. And the last time we kissed, he ghosted me. Not safe.

I jump off the counter. "Sorry. I lost my head. I haven't been kissed like that in a long time."

Honestly, I've never been kissed like that ever. Maybe because I've never shared a kiss with someone who made me feel known and understood.

I head to my bedroom. "Good night."

"Wait, Meg."

I turn, but I stay right where I am. The feel of his hands on my back still lingers, and if I get too close, I might do something drastic to get them there again.

"We are friends, right?" he asks. "No more blocking numbers or avoiding each other? We'll stay in contact? This kiss didn't ruin anything?"

His questions quiet some of my own fears. He wants to continue forward.

"We're friends."

He nods. "Good. Sleep well."

"You too."

I DON'T SLEEP AT ALL. A DANGER OF HAVING THE WORK schedule I do is sometimes when I should sleep, I can't.

Though this time, it might have more to do with my kiss with Noah than my wonky internal clock. Those minutes keep replaying in my mind. Over and over. It's disappointing to know it will never happen again.

Nothing like a romantic Christmas movie to get my mind off of my unromantic life.

I open the movie app and scroll through the options until I find one I haven't seen before. A second-chance romance. One of my favorite tropes.

It doesn't take me long to get sucked in. If Noah were awake, this stellar story arc would captivate even him. Or at least he'd grumble a lot less than with the other movies.

The characters are two best friends who have a falling out in college because of a misunderstanding. It's years later when they run into each other just before Christmas.

Because of unforeseen circumstances, they're stuck together for a few days in a cabin.

People who don't like romance tell me romance stories are boring because everyone knows how it will end: with a happily ever after. As much as I love a happy ending, what I love more is the journey the characters go through to get there.

And two people stuck in a small cabin with only one bed and very little to do but talk to each other and kiss is a fun journey.

It hits me quite abruptly ...

This is the story of Meg and Noah. Earlier, I found the perfect movies to describe Livy's adventures in Wyoming. Now I've found mine.

Two friends are torn apart by misunderstandings and then stuck together in a condo while the girl's family is sick with food poisoning.

Of course, Noah and I aren't meant to be together romantically. I'm glad we're just friends. It would be depressing to think we wasted eleven years apart when life would lead us right back to each other later on. So much wasted time.

Except, even as friends, we wasted time. Without Matt's meddling, I would've been at every one of Noah's ball games. I would've been there when he broke his wrist and helped him through the disappointment of giving up baseball. He would've been at my graduation from my nursing program. All those missed nights dancing, talking, and laughing together. All those wasted years make me heartbroken.

Second-chance romance may be romantic in the movies, but in real life, they suck.

Chapter Nineteen

NOAH

I sit on the end of the couch and stare at my phone screen. I've had five text messages and two missed calls from my dad within the last five hours. It's past midnight, but he's probably waiting up for me to return his call. I don't want to talk to him, but I don't want to disappoint him either.

I delete the voicemails and texts without reading them and push the call button.

"Hello?"

"Dad. I got your messages."

"Noah, your mom sent your Christmas gift to my place. She only sent it here so I would have to pay to have it forwarded to you. She knows you're with the *Wrights* for Christmas."

He says their name like it's a bad word, but it isn't like he wants me to visit over the holidays. He likes having time off from work and no responsibility.

I swallow my sigh. "I'll send you the money to have it sent to my hotel in Baltimore."

"Good. Next time you talk to your mom, tell her to stop sending your things here. It's an enormous box but weighs practically nothing. She just wants to torture me."

"Can you send me whatever is inside?" This shouldn't be as big of a deal as he makes it out to be.

"I guess so," he grumbles. A long pause. "How are you, anyway?"

"Great."

"Good. Stay out of trouble."

He ends our call. Talking to him on the phone is always shorter than when I talk to my mom. And he doesn't ask for money.

Even after I dispense with my duties as a son, I can't sleep. I blame it on Meg. That kiss. How am I ever supposed to look at her as a friend when I know she kisses like that? Half of me wishes she picked the shoe lick, the other half wants to kiss her again. But another kiss would make me want another and another. Her kisses are like Lay's potato chips. I can't stop at just one.

Neither can I ignore my desire to spend every waking minute with her. I don't want to leave for Baltimore in two days. I want to stay with her for as long as possible.

We do friendship well. In high school, we clicked right from the beginning. If I hadn't screwed things up, we might have become something more than friends.

That's what haunts me now. What would "more" look like? I want to find out, but I also don't want to lose what we have. If we did try dating, but then broke up down the road, could we get back to where we are now? Or would we go back to where we were two days ago? Is it worth the risk to find out?

"NOAH." I WAKE TO MEG WHISPERING MY NAME IN A SING-SONG voice. "Noooooah. No-no-no-no-noah."

It can't be morning yet. I swear I just fell asleep.

"What time is it?" I mumble.

"Six."

I don't think I fell asleep until after two. "Why are you waking me up at six?"

"Because I made you hot cocoa. Mmm, mmm, good."

I'd smile, but my lips are too tired to put forth any effort. "Real hot cocoa, or pretend hot cocoa?"

"It's the real deal."

She must wave the mug next to my face because I feel the steamy heat and smell watery chocolate.

I crack an eye. In the dim light cast by the hallway light, I see her kneeling in front of me; her face close to mine, two cocoa cups within reach.

"Cocoa is the reason I'm awake?" I ask.

"Only one reason. The second reason is so we can make gingerbread houses."

I groan. "At six in the morning? It's still dark outside."

"It's always dark outside. It's winter."

I don't have a counterargument, so I close my eyes. I'm almost asleep again when she pokes my side.

"Get up, sleepyhead. We have gingerbread houses to make."

"Come back in two hours."

"If we want to get them finished before Mom and I need the kitchen to make dinner, we have to start now. They need to refrigerate for a few hours. Please?"

I can't say no to her pleading and sit up reluctantly. After a huge yawn, I ask, "*Why* are we making gingerbread houses at six in the morning?"

She hands me a cocoa cup and moves to sit on the couch beside me. She snuggles in close and pulls my blanket over both of our laps.

"Six-oh-five," she says. "You've wasted precious minutes complaining about the hour. I'm usually getting home for work or arriving at work by this time in the morning."

"You're amazing," I say.

She takes a sip, and I follow her lead. I'd prefer coffee, but cocoa is still better than air.

"Thank you," she says with enthusiasm. Seriously, how is she so lively after our late night? "As to the reason for the gingerbread houses, in the movies the characters always make cookies. Houses sound more fun, and we can have a bake-off."

"What's a bake-off?"

"Haven't you ever watched *The Great British Baking Show*?"

I shake my head.

"It's a friendly baking competition."

I yawn again. "Our bet ended last night," I say, hoping to convince her I need more sleep, and we can dispense with the friendly baking competition.

"I've had so much fun, I thought we could keep going with our daily activities."

I lean my head on the back of the couch. It's too heavy to keep upright. "You mean pretending to be in a movie?"

"Yeah."

"A *romance* movie."

"Except ours is a friendship movie. They have those, you know."

"On the Hallmark channel?"

I feel her shrug and then lean away, as if she's suddenly aware she sat down so close she's practically on my lap. "Well ..."

Now is my chance to say what I spent hours thinking about before falling asleep. I brace myself. I have no idea what to expect from her, but I have to find out. Being afraid of confrontation kept me from speaking to her when we were teens. Not this time.

I sit up straight. "Meg, I like you."

She smiles up at me. "I like you too."

I take her hand and weave our fingers together. She doesn't pull away. That's a good start.

"I'm so glad we're friends again," I say. "I've missed you."

She nods. "Same. It's crazy how we could pick up our friendship like there wasn't a pause that spanned a decade."

"In high school, I hoped we would end up together," I say. "I wanted to ask you out for a long time, but I didn't have the courage until you kissed me."

"And then you took Vanessa to the Winter Ball." Her words come out as a growl.

"Matt convin—" I stop. I could blame it on Matt, but it was my choice to believe him instead of talking to Meg directly. I'll take responsibility for not taking responsibility at the time. "That email I wrote you senior year was me asking if you'd be my homecoming date."

"Really?" She looks down at our clasped hands.

"Yeah. Even after all these years, I can't help but think we could try again. There's no more miscommunication. No more lies. If you're up for take two, will you go out on a date with me Thursday night?"

She doesn't answer immediately. "The day after Christmas? But your flight leaves on Thursday."

"I'll change it."

Silence falls. She doesn't pull her hand out of mine, or stand up and stalk away. She sits, with her chin on her chest, and says nothing. The longer she doesn't answer, the more worried I become. Maybe all she sees for us is friendship, and she doesn't know how to let me down gently. That would be disappointing, but I could survive the disappointment as long as she was still in my life.

"Meg, if you only want friendship, that's okay, too."

She rubs the back of my hand with her thumb. "There's a romance movie trope called the second-chance romance. It's about two people who had a chance at love, but it didn't take the first time around. It isn't until they meet again years later that it sticks, and they get their happy-ever-after. But in real life, if two people were meant to be together, why did they spend so many years apart? It's sad, don't you think? Maybe they're only meant for friendship."

I won't pretend this isn't a roundabout way to ask about us. "I think it would be sadder if we never found our way back to each other at all."

"Oh, that's a good point. I hadn't thought about that." She leans her head against my arm. "I'm nervous. Friendship feels safe. After a few dates, we could fall apart again. I don't want to lose you."

"You won't. No matter what, we'll always be friends."

"How are you so sure?"

"Because I don't want to lose you either. I know what it's like to live without you, and I don't want to do that again. I'm scared too, Meg. My parents are not good examples of how to make a relationship work. I don't want to screw this up."

She takes a loud breath and blows it out between her lips. "So, you're asking for a date on Thursday?"

That was where the conversation started. "Yes, Thursday night."

"I'll get home from work around seven, and I can't stay out late because I work the next day."

I'm relieved she said yes and sink further into the couch. I release her hand so I can wrap my arm around her shoulders.

"I can agree to those terms," I say. "If all goes well, maybe we can go out on Friday night, too."

She snuggles into my side. "I have Saturday off, so we can stay out late. How about dancing? There's a country-western bar near my apartment."

I kiss the top of her head. She sighs.

"I don't have to be in Baltimore until after the new year. Do you work on January first?"

"Nope. I have the thirty-first off, too."

"Will you be my New Year's date?"

Before she answers, she giggles.

"Is that funny?" I ask.

"Not at all," she answers, but she keeps giggling.

"What? I don't understand the joke."

I laugh with her, but only because her laughter is contagious. I'm still confused.

"No joke," she finally says. "I'm just so happy. I feel like my heart is about to burst out of my chest. This is all so unexpected. How can a person go from dislike to like so quickly?"

"The magic of Christmas ," I say in all seriousness. "Those movies know what they're talking about."

Another round of giggles erupts. "I guess so."

"When you stop laughing, can I kiss you?"

"I'd be upset if you didn't."

When my lips touch hers, I feel whole, as if my life has finally fallen into place. If I had any worries about dating Meg, they're gone. I'm lost in the feeling of having her in my arms. No more scowls or misunderstandings between us.

I make myself stop kissing her, but only with great willpower.

"Tell me the plan for today, now that I'm awake," I ask.

"A friendly gingerbread house competition. You, me, my parents, and hopefully not Matt. Kitchen stuff really isn't his thing."

"Well, I can't say it's my thing either. I've never made cookies before."

She pulls back. "How have you gotten to be an adult without ever having made cookies? It's a rite of passage."

"Then I guess we'd better fix that." I tuck a strand of hair behind her ear. "If we're keeping up with our activities, maybe we can go ice skating? Just for an hour. The rink opens at nine."

I can't suppress my yawn. As much as I want another day with Meg, I'd like it not to start so early.

"I'll take pity on you," Meg says. She smacks a kiss on my cheek. "I'll make the dough while you get a little more sleep, and while it sits in the refrigerator for a few hours, we'll visit the ice rink and go buy candy for decorations. Does that work?"

I smile with relief. "Yes. Especially the part where I get a few more hours of sleep."

She kisses me and lingers before standing and taking a step backward. "I'll try to be quiet."

"I'm tired enough that I won't hear a thing."

I lay down, but even though I crave sleep, I also crave Meg. By the light of her phone, I watch her gather ingredients. There's a skip to her step and a smile on her lips. She's beautiful. Kind. Fun. Always up for a laugh. A great dance partner. I love everything about her.

We're dating. It feels like my teenage wish is finally coming true after all these years. This time, I won't screw it up.

Chapter Twenty

MEG

I FIND AN AMERICANIZED VERSION OF A PAUL HOLLYWOOD gingerbread house recipe and gather up the ingredients. Mom brought enough supplies for me to double the batch.

I can't keep the smile off my face. I dance around the kitchen, a skip to my step. Noah wants to date me. He isn't leaving the day after Christmas. He's staying with me for a week. My insides are fluttery. My thoughts jumbled. This is what it feels like to be on cloud nine.

I ignore the bit of concern I feel about Noah changing his mind like he did before. As a couple, we might not last the week, but no matter what, we will remain friends. Noah promised. That promise gives me the courage to give dating a try.

The overhead lights come on, and there's Mom, still in her nightgown.

"Meg, why are you up so early?"

"Noah is asleep. Can you turn off the lights?"

The lights flick off. "Sorry." She glances over at Noah's sleeping lump. "Poor Noah. We promised him a fun Christmas and then abandoned him."

No poor Meg. They abandoned me too.

"Noah and I have kept busy," I say. "I told you; we made amends. We've had fun together."

"Still, it isn't the Christmas either of you wanted. I'm sure Noah would've enjoyed the past few days if Matt weren't sick."

Based on the exuberance of Noah's kisses this morning, he's enjoyed the past few days with me. Mom wouldn't understand, because Matt is her golden child. I say nothing to contradict her perception of him.

"What are you doing up?" I ask.

Mom's a night owl. Mornings are torture. I'm surprised to see her before nine.

"I woke in a panic. I forgot to take the ham out of the freezer and put it in the fridge to defrost."

I point to the sink. "I took it out a few minutes ago. It should be defrosted by noon."

She comes around the counter to look in the sink filled with water and a ham. "Thank you. You've saved Christmas dinner. What are you up so early making?" She peers into the bowl.

"Couldn't sleep. I thought we could all decorate gingerbread houses this morning and have a friendly bake-off competition."

"That sounds fun, but we don't have any frosting or candy."

"Noah and I will go to the store."

She purses her lips. "Maybe you should wait until Matt's up before making plans. He might want to go skiing with Noah."

Right. Let's wait for Matt because he decides what everyone does, and I don't get a say.

I nod. "Okay." Not that I agree, just that I don't want to argue. There isn't a point. The third favorite child doesn't have a voice.

Mom yawns. "I'm going back to bed for a bit longer. You're okay?"

"Yep."

After she leaves, I lean back against the counter, feeling deflated.

"Are you alright?"

Noah's voice startles me. In the dark, he's a black lump on the couch, and I thought he was asleep.

"You heard all of that?" I ask.

"Yeah."

"Why didn't you say something? You could've told my mom how much you want to spend the day with me and not ski with Matt."

"I thought it was a good chance for you to tell her how you feel when she dismisses you. I didn't want to interrupt."

"What's the point?" My voice sounds as sad as I feel. My happiness from minutes ago is gone. "She doesn't listen when I do speak up. You heard how I told her we had fun, but she still thinks you must be miserable because Matt wasn't available to entertain you."

"If you don't talk, she has nothing to listen to."

"If I don't talk, then I don't give her the opportunity to ignore everything I say."

I'm glaring at him. By the light of my phone, I'm sure he can see. I, however, cannot see how he's looking at me, and I feel at a disadvantage.

He sits up. "Not talking to your parents has made it easy for Matt to make up a story about you that isn't true. I guarantee they don't mean to hurt you. They love you just as much as they love Matt."

"And if they don't care what I have to say?"

"Then keep trying until they do care."

"You make it sound easy."

"It's not. I get that. But don't give up."

I want them to see me as I really am, but the fear that they never will has held me back. Maybe Noah is right? Maybe I can carve out a place in the family that isn't in the forgotten attic.

"Okay," I agree. "But not today. After Christmas. We're having breakfast on Saturday before they drive back to Idaho Falls. I'll talk to them then."

"I'll be there, too, unless you want me to skip out?"

"No, come."

It will be helpful to have him as backup to what I have to say. I'm afraid my parents won't believe anything that contradicts what Matt has told them without a second witness.

Chapter Twenty-One

NOAH

I STAND ON THE EDGE OF THE ICE-SKATING RINK, WHICH IS A frozen pond they've smoothed over to give a false sense of security, and wonder what I've gotten myself into.

"Come on," Meg says from in front of me. She's on the ice and hasn't fallen. I'm impressed by her ability to balance on two thin blades. "This was your idea."

"Yeah, because I found it listed on a Hallmark Movie Bingo sheet. I haven't actually ice skated before. Are you sure it's safe? What if I fall and crack my head open?"

"Then I'll rush you to the emergency room."

"That's down in the valley. What if I fall through the ice at the same time and come down with hypothermia?"

"Then I'll strip off all your clothes, wrap you in my coat, and drive you to the emergency room."

I can't help but smile at that visual. "You would like that, wouldn't you?"

She blushes. "You realize I'm a nurse, right? If you're hurt, I can help. Besides, you had baseballs thrown at your head all the time. Why are you afraid of falling on ice?"

"I wore a helmet when those balls were being thrown, and I had a bat to hit them back. This is a completely different situation."

She looks over to the skate rental booth. "They have helmets here if you'd like one. They're for kids, but I'm happy to see if they have a double extra-large to fit on your colossal head. We can also get you ski poles to hit the ice before it hits you."

I scowl. "Now you're just being mean."

"I'm trying to help," she laughs. "If you don't want to ice skate, we don't have to ice skate. We can go get ice cream instead."

"You and ice cream."

"It's a winter staple."

The bantering helps distract me from what I'm about to do. I take a step onto the ice, then another. Meg holds onto my hands to help steady me.

"Push off with your right foot," she says.

I give the tiniest push and glide forward. The top half of my body wavers like a flag in the wind, but Meg's hold keeps me standing.

"Now your left."

Another tiny push forward, and more gliding.

"This isn't so bad," I say.

I should have held onto those words. In the next second, my blade hits a rough spot. I flail forward, then lean back to find my balance, but don't find it until I land on my butt.

I look up at Meg as she laughs.

"You let go of me," I say.

"Because I would have fallen on top of you. I saved you an elbow in the ribs." She holds out a hand. "Now that you've fallen once, you know it's no big deal. Kind of like skiing."

"My bruised butt cheek doesn't agree." Or my bruised ego. "People actually think this is fun? And romantic? Those Christmas movies have it all wrong."

"Come on, let's try again."

She holds out her hands, but I don't want to pull her down with me, so I roll over to my knees and put one foot down while the other knee is on the ice before I take her offered help.

"This time," she says, "Keep your knees bent and lean forward to keep your center of gravity balanced."

"Information that would have been helpful five minutes ago."

"I didn't realize you would be so bad at this."

I'll be bruised from that tumble, and probably from all the times I will fall in the next hour, but I don't care. I'm with Meg. She's happy, and when I fall and scrape my palm on the ice a minute later, she kisses it better.

I DON'T LAST ON THE ICE LONGER THAN TWENTY MINUTES. BY then, I don't think there's an inch of me that won't turn black and blue by tomorrow.

"We are never going ice skating again," I say.

"You can get better with practice. You made it two minutes without falling at the end."

"I'm a hopeless case. Let's give up and not waste the time."

She shakes her head at my tantrum but gives me an indulgent smile. "If you say so."

After we return our skates, I tug her in the opposite direction as the lodge.

"I have one more errand to run," I say.

She glances at her phone for the time. "I'm sure the groceries we bought have been delivered by now. We have gingerbread houses to decorate."

"Later. Right now, I'm worried about not having a Christmas present for you."

"What do you mean? You give me a gift card every Christmas."

"Yeah, for twenty bucks. That's a relic from when we didn't talk to each other. Now we're something completely different, and I can't give my girlfriend a movie ticket."

Meg stops in the middle of the sidewalk.

I turn to face her. "What?"

"Girlfriend?" she says.

"Isn't that what we talked about this morning?"

"Yeah, but it sounds so official."

I look down at our clasped hands. "I hope we're official. I don't know what you think the last two days have been, but for me, it's the start of something wonderful. Something I've wanted since the day you smiled at me in English class. Now that we're together, I don't want to waste time pretending otherwise."

Her eyes glisten. She's too beautiful not to kiss, so I kiss her. She kisses me back with a fervor I can get used to. We make it short. We are in the middle of a busy sidewalk.

"Now that we have that worked out," I say, "I need to get my girlfriend something for Christmas. Will you help me pick it out?"

"What did you have in mind?"

"Let me show you."

I lead her past a few more shop doors until we reach the bookstore.

"Books?" she asks as she looks up at me.

"Is that okay? As many as you want."

"As many as I want? You shouldn't say things like that. New books average twenty dollars a piece. What if I wanted ten?"

I shrug. "Okay."

"Fifteen?"

"Sure."

Her eyes widen. "Fifty?"

"You'd really want fifty books? It would take you twenty-five years to read them all."

She bites her lip and tries to stifle her laughter. "Not quite. I read one or two books a week. But even then, it isn't all about reading the books I own. It's about looking at them on my bookshelf and the anticipation of reading them. Sometimes the anticipation lasts for years before I crack the cover. I have a whole bookcase full of pretty books I haven't read yet, and I love every one of them."

My eyes get wider with every sentence. "That makes no sense."

"Because you aren't a reader. It makes perfect sense on Bookstagram."

I latch on to the part of this conversation that makes sense. "Two books a week for the next year. That's one-hundred, four books." I wave to the door of the bookstore. "Let's go pick them out."

She takes a step back and tugs on my hand to keep me from entering.

"That's over two-thousand dollars!" Her voice is practically a screech. "You cannot spend that much money on me."

"Meg," I say with all seriousness. I need her to understand that I'm not teasing. "I live in hotels my company pays for. They buy my food, cover all travel expenses, and even give me a stipend each year to buy really expensive suits. I have no one to spend money on but myself. Please, let me spoil you. Let me buy you a Christmas present that shows how much I adore you."

She tries to keep her stubborn glare, but it melts away. "Okay. Ten books."

"Fifty," I counter.

"Nine."

"Forty."

"Five."

"That isn't how negotiations work." I move us inside the building so we aren't blocking the door. "I'm going down. You need to go up so we can meet in the middle."

"Really?" She raises her eyebrows. "Because I'm pretty sure this way worked for you on Sunday when you tricked me into ten activities a day."

I can't help but give in to her logic. "Fine. Ten books."

"Thank you." She steps around me and leads the way to the back.

"At least to start," I say as I follow behind.

She turns and walks backward. "You're the worst."

"I'd like to argue I'm the best."

We get to the romance area. After glancing around to see if anyone is nearby, Meg pulls me down to her level and touches her lips to mine.

"I concede. You're the best." She kisses me again. "At being the worst."

It's only been a few hours, but I can already anticipate that dating Meg will never be dull.

Chapter Twenty-Two

MEG

NOAH FOLLOWS BEHIND ME AS I BROWSE THE SHELVES. WITHIN a few minutes, I pull out five books I've been wanting to read. Noah holds them as I scan the backs of a few others. When I turn to add another to my growing pile, there are two books I didn't put there.

"Where did these come from?" I ask.

Noah shrugs. "I liked the covers. They don't count toward your ten. They're bonuses."

I love today too much to argue. A handsome, generous man wants to buy me books and kiss me breathless between the rows of a bookstore? Yes, please.

When we get to the checkout a half hour later, Noah carries seventeen books. I made sure half of them are used books, but still, that is one pricey Christmas gift.

He won't let me take a bag as we walk back to the lodge.

He's my pack mule. I loop my arm through his and lean into his side.

"Thank you, Noah. I love all my books."

"Good." Then he grimaces. "That puts the pressure on for next year. And your birthday. Maybe I should have started off with a meager three books and added on every year. The way it is now, inflation is going to be steep."

He winks, and I laugh. A year with Noah as my boyfriend sounds magnificent, but the niggling doubt in the back of my head makes me wonder if he even needs to worry about gift inflation. What if, once again, I like him more than he likes me?

I swallow my doubts. Those are worries for a different day.

MATT AND DAD AREN'T AT THE CONDO WHEN WE RETURN from my book-shopping spree.

"They went skiing," Mom tells us as she chops cauliflower for tonight.

Of course, they did. I'm not sad Matt isn't here, but I am disappointed Dad didn't want to decorate a house with us. I've hardly seen him since dinner on Friday night.

"Noah," Mom says, "They didn't leave long ago. You can catch up. Just be back by a little before six, so you have time to change before dinner and gifts."

"No," Noah says with a shake of his head. "I want to stay here. Meg and I are making gingerbread houses."

Mom's face scrunches in confusion as she glances

between the two of us. "Are you sure? Matt really wanted to ski with you today. Meg can make a house on her own."

Thanks, Mom.

I busy myself with unpacking the grocery bags that were delivered. Though I don't look at Noah, I know he's waiting for me to say something before he answers my mom. What am I supposed to say? About how Matt decides everything? About how I feel like the spare child? About Noah's upgraded status to my boyfriend?

I don't know where to start or even what to say. There's no reason to argue on Christmas Eve.

"I'm sure," Noah finally says. "We're having our own cooking show."

I cannot suppress the happiness that bubbles up inside at Noah's enthusiasm. He picks me. And though there isn't a competition between me and Matt for Noah's affection, it feels that way. I won this round.

"Oh. Okay." Mom's confusion is obvious. She puts the cauliflower into a plastic food container and sticks it into the fridge. "Well, I've prepared a few things for dinner, but Meg, the ham goes in the oven at noon and we'll need to get started on everything else around two."

"Sounds good." That gives us three hours for houses. Plenty of time. I swap Mom places and grab the dough from the fridge. "Shall we get started?"

"Not me," Mom says apologetically. "I have a few people to call about the New Year's party I'm planning. One of our vendors backed out this morning."

Mom heads off to her bedroom, leaving us alone.

Noah claps his hands once and then rubs them together. "Where do we start?"

And so I give Noah his very first baking lesson. We roll the dough, cut the pieces from a template I make from the lodge stationary, and bake them. Because I made a double batch, we have enough left over to cut out gingerbread men to hang on the tree.

It takes longer to get everything in the oven than it should because of all our kissing breaks. It's like we have eleven years to catch up on, and we're both game to do it all in one day. I really don't mind the delay, but my mom expects the kitchen clear for dinner prep, so I make the breaks quick.

Besides the kissing, it's incredible being with Noah. He's funny and kind. And obtuse. I try to explain the concept of *The Great British Baking Show*, but he refuses to understand.

"The premise of the show makes little sense," he argues. "Why would anyone compete in timed cooking trials? They're trying to make baking a sport, and it isn't a sport."

"It's fun."

He huffs out a breath as he places another man on the cookie sheet. "One day of this is fun. Ten weeks of weekends spent in a tent kitchen? That sounds like a punishment for something horrific I've done in a previous life."

"I'm going to make you watch a season."

"How about just one episode?" he counter offers.

"We'll start with one episode, but once you get a taste for the show, you'll be the one begging to watch the entire season."

"Do you want to make a bet?"

I see the glint of competition in his eye, and I decide this is another bet he'll make sure I lose. "No, thank you."

Once the cookies are all cut out, we make a big bowl of frosting.

"Meg, you have some powdered sugar on your cheek."

I rub my cheek against my shoulder to wipe it clean.

"Still there," Noah says. "Let me help."

I turn to face him, and in one fluid motion, he dips his finger in the frosting bowl and wipes it on my cheek.

"Noah!"

"What? Fighting with food happens in all the movies. Google told me so."

In that case, I grab a handful of flour and throw it at his face. He's taller than I am, and most of it falls back on me. I cough at the flour cloud. He has the gall to laugh. The meany.

I grab a handful of M&M's, pull open the waistband of his jeans an inch, and drop them down his pants.

"What!" he yells like they're ice cubs and not harmless chocolate candies.

He shakes his hips and a few pings sound as candy falls to the floor. His jeans are snug, so most of them are still stuck in his pants. Before laughter can overtake me, I have the frosting beaters in hand and rub them down his arms.

"You play dirty!" he says.

"I watch a lot more movie food fights than you do."

He forgets about his candy pants and backs me up against the counter. His hands go on either side of me. I think we've earned another kiss, but instead, he reaches into the bowl and covers his finger with white, fluffy frosting. A dollop lands on my nose. Then my lips. The frosting is cold against my skin.

"What are you doing?" I ask.

"My version of a food fight."

He gets more and paints my cheeks. His touch is soft, almost like a caress. Then he adds M&M's to the frosting all over my face. It's not such a bad way to fight with food.

I turn away laughing and dip my finger in the bowl to return the favor. I give him a frosting mustache, then begin work on a full beard.

"You look good with white hair," I say. I open the package of Neccos and add them to his cheek. "No need to worry about how you'll age."

"You always look stunning."

He presses his lips to my forehead. The only spot on my face previously free of frosting is now covered in the stuff. Next, he kisses my lips.

"You taste sweet," he says.

I hold on to his shirt with both hands to keep his lips on mine for a little longer.

"The houses are probably cool enough to decorate," I say, before kissing him again.

"Okay."

I pull back, but not far, because I use his shirt to wipe off the frosting from my face.

"You must not mind my cologne anymore," he says.

"It's grown on me like mold on leftovers in the fridge. Kind of like you."

"You're so poetic."

"You bring out the best in me. Come on, let's get decorating. Mom will be in here soon to use the kitchen."

"I need to change. Maybe take a quick shower. Be back in a few."

The tinkling sound of falling M&M's follows him to the bathroom.

I'm laughing as I splash water on my face and wash off the remnants of the frosting fight. This is the kind of life I could get attached to very easily.

NOAH'S GINGERBREAD HOUSE WILL FALL WITH THE SLIGHTEST nudge. There are gaps between the walls and roof and not enough icing to hold up the Neccos he used as shingles. He outlined the door and windows with pull-and-peel Twizzlers and put mini M&M's, at least those that survived the "food fight," all over the outside walls. It looks like it has chicken pox. I don't think he's even trying at this point, but he's having fun.

He goes to the desk and grabs a sheet of hotel stationery and rolls it into a tube, one side wider than the other, then rummages through the box of gift-wrapping supplies Mom brought until he finds tape.

I put the last spice drop along the edge of my M&M cobbled path. My house is adorable. Especially when compared to Noah's shack.

"Who's going to judge?" he asks.

"Instagram. I'll take a picture of each and post a poll. Whoever gets the most votes in the next few hours, wins."

"Sounds fair, but only if you don't say which one is yours. They are your friends."

I glance at his leaning house. Yep, no way my friends will know which one is mine if I don't tell them.

"Okay," I agree.

I pull out my phone to take a picture of each, before waving Noah over. "We need to take a picture of us with our houses."

"Mine isn't done yet," Noah says as he comes back to the table. "Give me one second."

He uses his index finger and pushes against the side wall of his house. It all comes tumbling down.

I gasp. "Noah!"

He is not disturbed in the slightest. He takes the paper, adds a bit of frosting to the narrower side of the tube, and attaches it to the roof of the collapsed house.

"What is that?" I ask.

"Guess."

I study the mess for a second, and then it hits me. A tornado. A tornado tore down the walls of his house.

I burst out laughing. Noah is full of surprises. His ugly T-shirt, the clown tree, and now this.

When my laughter dies down, I realize I have one arm around his back and my other hand lays flat against his abs. His arm is behind me, his hand warms on my hip. I don't remember moving to this spot. After so long apart, why does it feel so right to be near him?

"Are you going to take a picture of my house?" His voice is soft.

I'm not ready to let go. "In a second."

Chapter Twenty-Three

MEG

NOAH IS MORE OF A HINDRANCE THAN A HELP AS WE MAKE Christmas Eve dinner. I have to wonder if he's ever followed a recipe before. He's great at washing potatoes and grating cheese, but the pie filling is a mystery to him. As is the au gratin cheese sauce for the cauliflower. We have to start over after he scalds the milk.

Mom and I don't mind. I enjoy watching the effort. My dad and Matt are never in the kitchen, and it's fun to witness Noah give meal prep a try.

We spend the time laughing and talking. Noah gives me covert touches when Mom isn't looking. He even kisses the point where my neck meets my shoulder when she's rummaging in the fridge for a pint of cream.

I'm not sure why we're keeping our relationship a secret. It's nothing we've decided together. I just don't know how to tell Mom, and Noah's following my lead. I hope he doesn't think I'm ashamed or want to keep this under wraps. Because truthfully, I want to go out on the deck and yell out to everyone that Noah is my boyfriend. Just as long as my parents can't hear.

At five o'clock, Mom sends us from the kitchen to go get changed for dinner.

"Matt and Calvin will be back soon, and they'll want to shower before dinner. It'll be easier if you guys are out of the bathroom when they arrive."

We go our separate ways, and I check the status of our gingerbread house votes on Instagram. I'm ahead, but only by two. I told everyone this was a bake-off and to channel their inner Paul Hollywood, but it seems no one listened. They like the off-beat, unexpected shack over the respectable, upright house. I can't say I blame them.

My phone chimes with a text from my coworker.

Telesa: *Hey! A few of us are going out to get a drink tonight after our shift for some Christmas Eve cheer. Do you want to come? Doug will be there.*

Doctor Doug. I haven't thought of him once in the last two days, which is remarkable since he took up so much of my headspace before.

Meg: *I don't think so. I'll be getting home late, and I work the early shift tomorrow.*

Telesa: *Just in case here's the address.*

After my shower, I take my time getting ready. I've had Noah to myself for three days, and now I have to share. Will I go back to being the interloper in my own family, or will I have someone on my side? I'm nervous to find out.

When I'm ready, dressed in my pink dress with my hair curled and make-up ready, I head to the kitchen. I stop just outside the living area where no one notices me. Everyone is dressed up. Mom wears a beautiful navy blue, knee-length dress. Matt and Dad are in slacks and button-down shirts. The three of them stand together, talking about the slopes.

It's Noah who takes my breath away. His suit shows off his lean frame, the top button on his shirt undone. I never knew a patch of skin could look so sexy. I really want to kiss the hollow of his throat.

Not an appropriate thought for a family dinner.

He stands to the side, watching my parents and Matt talk, a wistful expression on his beautiful face. I wonder what he's thinking. Does he miss Matt? The idea sends an icy shiver down my spine.

"Merry Christmas!" I say as I enter.

"Merry Christmas," Mom and Dad say together.

Matt looks over and smiles. It's the smile he gives me all the time, the one that says, *my little sister is here and she's so adorable.* I don't trust that smile anymore. If he thinks ignoring what he did is going to make it disappear, he will soon discover he's mistaken.

Noah's eyes follow me as I walk across the room. I want to go to him, but I resist. I don't want Matt to sneer, nor do I want to take the time to convince Mom and Dad that it's an excellent decision for us to date. Tonight is our family Christmas. We have one evening to be all together. No wasting it.

"Shall we eat?" Mom says.

Once we dish up and sit, everyone digs in. Dad's Christmas jazz music plays. Lit candles are placed along the middle of the table. The lights are dim. It's an elegant, relaxing meal.

When the conversation turns toward how Noah kept busy while Matt was sick, he shares all the things we did. He invites me into the conversation by asking for my opinion and gives me an opportunity to contribute. It's nice being on the inside.

Of course, there's no mention of our bet, his argument with Matt, or the way he was kissing me against the counter earlier.

"I'm glad to see you two getting along," Dad says to us. "I've never liked the animosity. Now we're a happy family."

Matt glowers down at his plate. Yep, just one big, happy family.

Once we're finished with dinner, Mom and I clear the table and join the other three near the tree. Noah sits on the couch and pats the cushion next to him. I think I should probably sit somewhere else, but my addiction to being near him is strong, and I don't resist.

Matt's eyes narrow as he takes us in. He doesn't like seeing us together.

As tradition dictates, we always open gifts one at a time, all from the same person, with Mom and Dad going first.

Dad hands the three of us a small wrapped box, about the size of a book. It's light and when I shake it I hear something hit the sides.

"They're all the same," Mom says. "Make your guesses and then open them together."

Guessing on what is inside each gift is another tradition. When it comes to Mom and Dad's presents, I'm usually wrong.

"An envelope of money?" I say.

"A new phone?" Matt's guess is wishful thinking. The box isn't heavy enough to be a phone.

"A subscription to a meal delivery service." Noah gets the most points for creativity.

Mom's eyes glow with excitement. She's definitely a person who loves giving people gifts.

We rip them open together, then slip the lid off the box. It's a ticket for a cruise to the Bahamas in September.

"We thought it would be fun to go away as a family," Mom says.

Dad joins in. "The three of you are busy, and it's hard for us to be together all at once. This way we're stuck on a boat and there are no excuses not to have family time."

I don't know how to feel about this gift. I want to go on a cruise, especially with my parents, but with Matt? This trip might be extremely awkward and not at all the vacation our parents have in mind.

When none of us respond to the gift, Dad says, "Well, don't you want to go?"

Noah is the first to speak. "Judy, Calvin, this is too much."

Mom leans forward and pats his knee. "Not at all. You're family. It wouldn't be the same if you weren't there."

Dad nods in agreement. "We put our vacation out far enough that you should all be able to get off work. Matt? Meg?"

I glance toward Matt and he nods at me, as if he's giving me permission to go, even though we're in the middle of an argument. *Thanks, bro.*

I get up and hug Mom and Dad. "This is a wonderful gift. Thank you so much."

Noah is the oldest, so he hands out his gifts. He gives

Matt the newest generation of Air Pods. My mom receives diamond earrings and Dad silver cufflinks. For someone who believes Christmas is too focused on material objects, Noah knows how to give expensive gifts.

I get the standard twenty-dollar gift card. This year, it makes me smile because I have seventeen books in the back of my car waiting for my next day off.

When Matt gives me my gift, I know what it is, even without the scent of vanilla. He has a four-year rotation for me. This year is an expensive bath and body lotion set. A ten-minute trip to the mall, and he can check my name off his list.

I shake it, pretending ignorance. "The pan set on my Amazon wish list."

Matt laughs as if what he picked out for me is so much better than what I actually want. I tear through the professional wrapping job to reveal the expected gift. At least the vanilla scent is better than the last scent he gave me.

"Thank you, Matt," I say as the dutiful daughter I am.

Dad guesses golf balls as his gift. He never puts in a genuine effort in guessing, and it shows. Real gift: an old-fashioned shave set with more bottles than I know what they're used for.

Mom's gift is heavy. "I think it's a dutch oven," she says. Real gift: a red enamel dutch oven.

I don't know how Mom does it every year, but she is right ninety-five percent of the time. When I was a kid, I was sure she unwrapped gifts late at night when we were all asleep, then re-wrapped them before we woke up. How else could she know what was in a sealed box?

For years, I set boobie traps. Strands of hair under the

tape. Doodles on the edges of the paper. They were intact on Christmas morning. One year I gave a gift with two layers of wrapping paper and put glitter between them. She found that surprise on Christmas morning and was not happy.

Mom oohs and ahhs over her new bakeware. "I've been wanting to make sourdough bread from a starter. This is perfect, Matt."

"I remembered," he says proudly.

Matt can be sweet. It's what kept me believing for so long that he cared about me.

Matt gives Noah a personalized poker set with his name emblazoned on top of the case.

"For our next guy's trip," Matt says.

Matt's glance cuts in my direction for one second as the corner of his lips tip up as if he has this great secret he's proud of sharing with only Noah. But I already know the next guy's trip will be here in two months. His secrets aren't so secret anymore.

My gifts are the only ones left to give. I grab them from under the tree, careful to tear off the tags before I hand them out. I have two gifts for Matt, but I only give him the largest package. The smaller one I hand to Noah, along with his wrapped socks.

"Mom," I say, "Why don't you open yours first?"

She bounces the box in her hands a few times, then shakes it. "It's light. Quiet. I think it's a sweater."

When she removes the lid, it is indeed a sweater. A soft wool in red. She takes it gently from the box. "This is beautiful. Where did you get it?"

"Layla started an Etsy shop this year."

"She knitted this?"

"Yep. She always has knitting needles in her hand."

Livy and I bought most of our Christmas gifts from her in support. She's been saving money like mad, though neither of us has got a straight answer out of her on why. She'll tell us when she's ready. Until then, we pretend patience.

Dad shakes his package none too gently. "A tea cozy."

It, too, is a sweater, but in a cardigan style. It's thicker and has chunky buttons down the front.

"Your turn, Matt."

He's enthusiastic about opening the box. I always try to get him something special each year, but not anymore. He opens his gift to find a soft, knit blanket in black, his favorite color.

"Thanks, Meg. This is beautiful."

He pulls it out and looks at the bottom of the box. Then shakes the blanket. His confusion and disappointment are priceless. I may have bragged over the last few months about getting him something he would love. The blanket does not live up to the hype.

"Noah," I say with enthusiasm. "Your turn."

Noah shakes his first gift. It doesn't make a sound. "Dare I guess a sweater?"

It's the gaudy Christmas socks. He bursts out laughing. "These are awful." He glances over. "I love them."

"Now the other one."

The second box holds a concert ticket.

"Mick Ease and the Nomads' reunion tour?" He looks at me in awe, then glances at Matt.

Matt's face is white. His lips flat like a drawn line. I think it's obvious to both of them I swapped their gifts.

"How did you get this ticket?" Noah asks. "They sold out in less than five minutes."

"I know a person."

His grin grows. "Yeah?"

"Me," I say with a little bounce, my excitement uncontainable. "I'm the person I know. I have really fast fingers and my credit card information memorized." I laugh with giddiness. I'm proud I scored two tickets. It's close to a miracle. The venue is tiny and the interest is extreme. I've been holding this secret for months, and now I finally get to share it with someone. And that someone is Noah.

"I have the other ticket," I say. "Are you free in March to go with me?"

Noah laughs. "Yeah. I will be there."

Mick Ease and the Nomads have been my favorite band since I was thirteen. It devastated me when they broke up seven years later. I shared my love with Noah when we were friends. We'd spend hours in my bedroom doing homework and listening to their "Easy Made Hard" album on repeat.

Obviously, I didn't buy the ticket for Noah. Matt became a huge Mick Ease fan during our junior year in high school when they made it to the top of the Billboard charts. (He swears he's been a fan since they started, but it's a lie). When I first heard about their reunion tour, I knew Matt would love to go. I feel stupid now for imagining his excitement when I revealed I had a second ticket. As if he would exclaim, *Alone time with Meg! Yay!*

I ignore my brother and start singing Mick's most popular single, "Perfection." Noah joins in. It's more speaking the words than singing, but I'll take it. In three months, we'll be singing with Mick, Steve, Vaughn, and Eliot in person. I can't wait.

"Meg," Mom says, loud enough to be heard over our singing. We stop immediately. She sounds upset. "What about Matt's ticket? It's his favorite band."

I glance at Matt. His head is about to explode from jealousy.

"I only have two tickets," I say with a shrug. "Matt will have to get his own."

"How?" Matt says bitterly. "Even the resellers are sold out. I've tried to get tickets, and I can't. I have to go to this concert."

This situation is a perfect example of how well I know Matt, and how little he cares about me. If he were the one who scored two tickets, he would never think to give me one. If he had thirty Mick Ease tickets, I wouldn't even make the list.

If Matt hadn't gotten sick, I never would have spent time with Noah and found out the truth. Matt would have that ticket, and he knows it. Am I a petty person to be glad he feels pain because of his actions? If so, I don't care.

"Meg, why don't you give your second ticket to Matt?" Dad says. "He loves this band and you know how much it means to him."

"Yeah," Mom says. She even claps a few times to show her enthusiasm for this plan. "That's perfect. Noah and Matt can go together."

Dad's idea is not perfect. It's horrible. This concert is for me. Why can't my parents stand up for me as well as they do Matt? Why do they give Matt everything he wants?

"I am not giving up my ticket," I say. "I bought them, and I get to choose who uses them."

"I don't understand what's going on here," Mom says. She glances between the three of us with confusion. "Meg, you really want to go to a concert? And with Noah?"

"Yes, I do."

"I should go," Matt says in exasperation. "They're my favorite band."

"Matt has tried for months to find some way to get to this concert," Dad says. "What's the harm in giving him the extra ticket?"

I lose it. This is why I don't speak up. It's hard being heard when three people insist on putting me in a box and not letting me out.

Admittedly, this situation is my fault. I should have saved the ticket for later, when I was alone with Noah. The thrill of rubbing it into Matt's face was too great to resist.

"No." My one word is as loud as a clap of thunder. "You're not taking this from me."

"Meg," Dad starts, but I don't let him finish.

"It's my ticket. It's not extra. Since their first single, I have been a diehard fan of Mick Ease."

I want to reign in my frustration, but it's impossible. I've reached my breaking point. There is no holding back the flood.

"I've bought every album. I have every song memorized. I have a whole collection of biographies about them." I stand and stare them all down. "I made sure I had the day off when the tickets for this concert went on sale. I practiced the keys strokes on my phone to be sure I got in the second the box office opened." Each time I say "I," I poke myself in the sternum. I'll probably have a bruise. "My ticket is not extra. It's *my* ticket. Matt doesn't get *my* ticket. And my second ticket is Noah's. It's my gift to him. Don't you dare take it, Matt. I know you're thinking about swindling him out of it, and you can't."

My family looks at me like I'm a stranger. I haven't lost my temper like this since I was a kid. They probably thought I'd outgrown tantrums. Me, too. Apparently not.

"But Meg," Dad says. "You don't like concerts."

I am a stranger to my family.

Noah catches my eyes and mouths, "Tell them."

Our conversation from this morning comes to mind. *It's easy for Matt to lie because you don't tell them the truth.*

"It's okay," Matt says. "I don't have to go." He shakes his head at me the tiniest bit. He doesn't want our parents to know he's a liar.

I'm more concerned about ruining Christmas. I meant to hold off on this, but if I leave tonight without explaining, I'm afraid they'll never understand me. I want to be understood.

I take a deep, calming breath, then sit back down. "Why do you believe I don't like concerts?"

Chapter Twenty-Four

MEG

Mom and Dad share a look.

"Because concerts are loud," Dad says. "You don't like loud noises."

"And Matt tells us how anxious you get in large crowds," Mom says gently, like maybe we shouldn't be talking about this if it's a sensitive topic for me. "That's why his girlfriend came with us to Imagine Dragons last year when you said you didn't want the ticket we bought you."

"Ex-girlfriend," Matt mutters like that's the takeaway from what was just said.

I glare at my brother, but he won't meet my gaze.

I tell my parents, "I didn't know about any Imagine Dragons concert."

"Matt talked to you about it," Dad says.

"No, he didn't," I say. "If I had known, I would've gone. I

love concerts. That's one I would have enjoyed. Mom, I've told you about the concerts I go to with my friends."

Her eyes crinkle as she thinks. "Yes, but I just assumed they were smaller venues. And acoustic, so not loud." She turns her attention to Matt. "Why would you tell us she was anxious about going?"

"Because she told me," he says. He pulls his pant legs down and resituates himself on the couch. He shoots me a glance like it's my job to fall in line and back him up. "I don't know why she's pretending we didn't talk about this. She must've forgotten."

"Believe me," I say, "If you had ever called me to chat about anything, I would remember because it's never happened before."

Mom and Dad look between me and Matt, both of them confused. Noah reaches over and lays his hand over mine. After that, they look between all three of us. Now is my chance to give my story. No matter what, I know Noah believes me. Right now, that seems like enough.

I don't know where to begin, so I start with today. "I originally bought the Mick Ease ticket for Matt. I give gifts to show love. This week, I found out that he's been lying to me, to all of us actually, and I no longer want to give gifts to someone who dislikes me so thoroughly."

"Matt," Mom says. "Why does your sister think you don't like her? What lies?"

"I'm going to the party downstairs," he says. "I'll catch you later."

He stands and moves to leave, but Dad blocks his way. "Sit down. None of us are going anywhere until we figure out what's going on. We're a family. We support each other. Answer your mother's question."

Matt is the first to back down. He sits slouched with his arms crossed over his chest. "Meg thinks I don't like her because I don't like tattletales."

"And I don't like liars," I say. "Especially when they lie about me."

"Explain," Dad says. "Both of you."

I don't want to blame everything on Matt. Noah's right. This situation is also my fault.

"I'm not who I was as a twelve-year-old," I say. "I've grown up and changed, and I feel like you only see me as you did when I was a kid. You still rely on what my therapist said fifteen years ago. I know myself now. I know what I need. And I don't feel you trust me when I speak up for myself. When I'm with the family, I'm overlooked and ignored."

"Oh, Meg. Of course, we trust you." Mom looks at Dad before continuing. "We thought you didn't want us hovering and worrying. We've stood back. You've always been independent, and we thought we were giving you the space you needed."

"I don't need space. I need to feel a part of the family."

Matt harrumphs.

"What do you have to say for yourself?" Dad asks him. "You've been lying to us? Why?"

Matt stares at me for a long time before speaking. "When we were kids, everything was about Meg. Her tantrums, the way she isolated herself, how she didn't like when we had parties at the house. You guys worried about her all the time. Even after that therapist told you she was fine, you still worried. I was the afterthought. I was the happy kid who didn't cause you any concern. It made me invisible."

He sits up and turns to my parents. "Yeah, I didn't like Meg. I was angry. She was oblivious to how she affected our family. She was selfish. I didn't want to spend time with her, but she wouldn't leave me alone. So, I lied."

Listening to my brother is opening a window into our childhood I never saw. While I've felt excluded because I'm different, he felt excluded because he didn't cause our parents any worry.

"We're not kids anymore and you still feel this way?" I ask.

"I like it better when you aren't around." He points to Noah. "And now you're stealing my best friend."

"You stole him first," I say, my frustration rising. "He was my friend until you lied to both of us to keep us apart."

"I was doing you both a favor," he says.

"You were doing yourself a favor," I counter.

Noah lifts his hand to silence our argument. "I'm not a possession. Guess what, I could have been both of your friends. If you'd given me a chance."

Matt points to our hands, still clasped. "Seems to me there's more going on there than just friendship."

After an hour of talking things through with our parents, I have to leave for home. Another storm is coming in tonight, and I want to be down the mountain before it hits.

I head to my room to change out of my dress and pack up.

Our conversation hasn't improved my relationship with Matt. If anything, he's angrier than ever before because Noah and I are dating. The bottom line is, he doesn't like me. That knife has yet to be removed from my back. I'm not ready to forgive. I'm not sure I will ever reach that point, but I do understand him better.

My parents are livid over all the lies he's told them through the years. They're especially upset about how he set Noah and me against each other.

At least my parents and I understand each other better. From now on, they'll ask me how I feel and what I want, and I'll be honest when they do.

Chapter Twenty-Five

NOAH

JUDY AND CALVIN ARE HAVING A QUIET CONVERSATION IN THE kitchen while I pack up a few stray items and stuff them in my suitcase for my trip down the mountain with Meg.

I wonder how the next three days will go here, just Matt with his two angry parents. He's never disappointed them like this before. I won't be surprised if they all head home early.

I wish it all could have waited to come out until after Christmas, just so there wouldn't be this animosity during the holiday. But I am glad that Meg and I aren't keeping our relationship status on the down low anymore. I felt like I was lying to Judy and Calvin, and they don't deserve that kind of treatment.

Once everything is packed, I sit on the couch and wait for Meg. I pull up a business book on my phone to read, but someone sits down on the opposite side of the couch.

"Noah," Matt says. "I'm sorry."

I don't look over. I don't respond. I keep reading.

"Did you hear me? I'm sorry I lied to you."

When I still don't respond, he keeps talking.

"In the beginning, I was doing what I thought was best for all of us. You were a nobody, and Meg wanted you to remain that way. You were never meant for a small life. A lie felt humane."

"Or maybe you lied because you didn't want to make your parents mad and you're a selfish jerk," I mutter. I remember what he said last night to me and Meg about his motivations.

After a beat of silence, he says, "In all honestly, yes. I can own that up until the selfish jerk part."

I snort. "Honesty? Do you know the definition of those words? They fit you to a T."

He doesn't engage but continues with his apology.

"It wasn't until after we left high school, that I discovered just how difficult it was to keep all the lies in motion. By that point, I didn't have much of a choice. My only other option was to come clean, and that sounded like a bad idea. We know how well that went today." He waves around the room as if conjuring up an image of earlier. "I felt bad, but the easiest path was forward. How horrible could my lies be when we were all happy? You're traveling all over the place saving businesses. I'm an outstanding salesman. Meg's living her dream here." He sighs. "I was wrong."

I stare at my phone but don't pretend I'm reading. There is no artifice in his voice or demeanor. I'm surprised. Matt is a good friend, but he has never been great at acknowledging his mistakes.

"Do you still think that no harm was done?" I ask.

He doesn't answer immediately. When he does, the words come slowly. "I've had a lot of time to think over the last two days. I've watched you and Meg together, and I *might* have been wrong to keep you apart."

I look over and glare.

"I was wrong, okay?" he says defensively. After a staring match, he deflates. His shoulders round inward, and his confidence falters. When he speaks again, he sounds contrite. "I was wrong about keeping you guys from being friends over the years and wrong to lie to our parents. Earlier today I realized I helped push Meg out of the family. It wasn't on purpose. I figured it was her choice. If she wanted to be involved with the family, wouldn't she have visited more often? At least, that's what I told myself." He leans back and rubs his face. "I never meant to manipulate either of you."

Silence stretches out between us as I chew on his apology. I want to believe him, but that doesn't mean I'm ready to forgive. "Our friendship started out as a lie."

"No, that is definitely not true. We were friends before I started ..." here he pauses. Swallows. Mutters, "Before I started using you to keep Meg away. Since then, we played ball together for seven years. We went to the same college. We've traveled all over the states. You have a room at my house to crash in between clients. All of that is outside of Meg."

This is true. Playing ball together in high school, we would've been friends anyway.

"Have you apologized to Meg?" I ask.

He shakes his head. "Not yet. I don't think she's ready to

listen, and I don't blame her. Maybe you could put in a good word for me?"

I snort. "I'll leave that to you. I'm not putting myself in the middle of your relationship with Meg. Besides, I haven't forgiven you yet."

He nods, but his expression is one of disappointment. "That's fair. But, um, I have a favor to ask."

Of course, he does. I brace myself. "What's that?"

"Stay through Saturday? Let me prove I'm a better person than you think I am. And, in full honesty, be a buffer between me and my parents. They still like you. I can't say the same for me right now."

I want to say no. He's lied to me for years, and it will take longer than three days for him to prove he's not the monster behind the mask. I also want him to hurt a little so he can get a taste of what Meg and I feel because of what he's done. Abandoning him would do just that.

Except ... Matt has seen me through a lot. With my parents, in work, in sports, and in life. He's never turned his back on me. The possibility of losing him as a friend hurts more than the pain of the lies he's told. As angry and as hurt as I am, I can't let the last few days ruin our friendship.

I nod. "Okay."

Matt collapses back into the couch. "Thanks, man."

Meg and I will still have next week together and our New Year's date. I hate that I'm disappointing her, but she'll be at work for the next two days. She won't even notice my absence.

At least that's what I tell myself.

Chapter Twenty-Six

MEG

I'M PACKED UP WHEN A SOFT KNOCK COMES AT MY DOOR. NOAH is on the other side. He opens his arms, and I lean into his embrace. I'm swallowed with warmth and the scent of his cologne I've come to love. I would be happy to stay here a while longer, but the winter storm is coming in fast.

"Are you ready to go?" I ask.

His arms tighten for one second before he pulls away enough to look down at me. "I need to stay with Matt."

I thought I was prepared for this possible eventuality, but I'm not. The disappointment is devastating and immediate.

"What?" I take a step back, and his grip loosens. "Why? After everything he's done to us, you want to stay?"

He rubs his wrist and won't meet my eyes for a few seconds. "He apologized. I haven't forgiven him, but I can't write him off completely. You have no idea what my parents have been like over the last few years, and he's been there with me through it all."

I would know exactly what his parents are like if Matt hadn't lied to keep us apart.

"He wants to apologize to you," Noah continues. "Whenever you're ready."

He'll be waiting a long time.

"I know we had plans this week," he says. "Can we postpone for a few days? I'm still staying in Salt Lake City next week."

That's what he says now, but after a few days with Matt, he could change his mind again. Persuasive, charismatic, manipulative, selfish Matt. It's like we're fighting over a favorite toy. I don't want to make Noah choose between us, but I also want him to choose me.

I hate that Noah is staying, but I refuse to show him just how much this hurts.

"Yeah, um, okay." I turn and zip up my suitcase so he can't see my face. "Can I hold on to the Mick Ease ticket for safekeeping? It'll help me worry less about it getting lost if I know where it is."

And I'll know that Noah won't hand it over to Matt anytime in the future.

"Sure." Noah takes it out of his wallet and holds it out to me. "I really am sorry. I'll miss you."

"I'll see you Saturday," I say. "That's not too far away."

It feels forever away.

My phone chimes with a text.

Dr Doug: *Meg! Telesa says you aren't coming tonight for drinks? I hope she's wrong. It won't be the same without you. I* *have the next week off so I won't see you until the new year if you bail on us! Please come.*

Doug is a flirt. Now that I've reconnected with Noah and know what it means to be with someone who is authentic, the tug this text would've had on me three days ago is gone. I feel nothing.

Noah glances down. "Is that the doctor you like working with so much?"

I slip my phone into my coat pocket without responding and grab my suitcase. "I better go."

Noah takes the suitcase from my hand. "I'll walk you down to your car."

When we come out into the living room, Mom and Dad are waiting. They pull me into a hug.

"We love you, Meg," Dad says. "We're sorry you haven't felt like part of the family."

"We'll all be better at communicating from now on," I say.

"Of course," Mom says. "We'll see you Saturday for breakfast."

"Is Matt in his room?" I'm glad that I don't have to pretend to care that I'm leaving him behind, but I am curious about where he went.

They share a disapproving look. "He is. He should be out here apologizing, but he said you probably wouldn't want to see him."

He'd be right.

Noah takes my hand as we exit the condo and doesn't let go until we're outside. Fat flakes have already begun to fall. The snow muffles everything, and I feel a little like I'm caught in a snow globe.

"I'll call you tomorrow," Noah says.

"You better. I'll be working, so I might not answer, but leave me a message, and I'll call you back."

"I'll text you then."

He helps me into the driver's seat, places my suitcase in the back, and scrapes my windows. Before I drive away, he kisses me softly.

"Be safe, Meg."

"Merry Christmas."

I pull out of the parking spot and look back in the rearview mirror as I drive away. He waves before he disappears from my view.

On the drive home, I'm filled with worry. Back in high school, the day Noah tried out for the baseball team, we kissed and made plans for the dance. Then he disappeared from my life. Eleven years later, I'm stuck in the same place. For less than a day, Noah and I had a chance. Now he's changed his plans to stay with Matt.

Matt always comes first.

I try to hold on to the hope I felt earlier today, but after years of coming last, I'm programmed to doubt.

When I reach my apartment, the windows are dark. Every other window has Christmas lights and people inside celebrating the holiday.

I don't want to be alone.

After a quick text to let my parents know I made it home, I pull out of my space and head to the bar to spend a few hours with my coworkers.

The bar isn't far. I hear the music from the parking lot. The party has spilled out onto the patio, and people huddle around heat lamps as snowflakes fall. Telesa, Doug, and the others are in a group laughing. They are dolled up for a party, and I second guess my jeans and sweater, but too late now.

Just as I get out of the car to join them, my phone dings with a text. For a second, I think it's Noah and my pulse picks up.

Dad: *Are you in for the night? Sleep well.*

I love my dad, but I'm still a bit disappointed it isn't my boyfriend.

Meg: *Out with some friends for a bit.*

Dad: *Don't stay out too late. You have work tomorrow.*

Such a dad thing to say. It doesn't matter that I'm twenty-seven and have been living out of his house since I was eighteen.

I send him a thumbs-up.

For a minute, I contemplate texting Noah, but in the end, decide not to. He wanted to stay with Matt, and I have to respect his space. In high school, Matt accused me of being clingy, and I don't want to prove him right.

I move to join my friends.

Telesa sees me first and screams a welcome while holding out her arms for a hug. She sloshes a little of her drink before she pulls away. It smells like pina colada, and now so do I.

"You came!" She yells in my ear. Someone has had too much to drink. "Merry Christmas!"

I'm swallowed up in the group. The hours pass away as we dance and sing along to the music. Because I work early tomorrow, I stick with club soda and head out just after midnight. Now that I'm exhausted, I'm ready for my empty, quiet, dark apartment.

"Good night!" I yell out to everyone.

"Love you!" Telesa screams back. It's a good thing they brought a designated driver.

Doctor Doug follows me out to the parking lot. "Wait, Meg. Who is that guy in all your Instagram photos?"

Is that a hint of jealousy in his voice?

"Um, my boyfriend."

Is it a lie to call Noah my boyfriend? It's only been a day, and he's already backed out of plans because of my brother. We could be something different by the weekend.

He clears his throat. "I didn't realize you had a boyfriend."

"It's a new development."

He looks into the distance. "Well, Merry Christmas."

"Thanks," I say. "You too. See you next year."

He heads back toward the group, but not before looking over his shoulder one last time. If I had to guess at his expression, I'd say he's disappointed I'm taken.

It gives my ego a gentle boost, but we both know there's nothing between us but loose friendship. My time with Noah has allowed me to disengage from my infatuation, and for that, I'm grateful. As nice as Doctor Doug is, I want a relationship that's deep and real.

I want Noah.

Chapter Twenty-Seven

MEG

In years past, I've enjoyed working on Christmas day. I enjoy offering cheer to patients and helping families deal with difficult situations during a time that should be full of joy.

This Christmas, I feel little cheer myself. I go through the motions, and think I'm doing a decent job of pretending, but I'm asked multiple times throughout my shift if I'm okay.

If Noah would text me, I would be. Better than okay. But nothing. Has he already forgotten me?

It's a long shift. Every hour feels like an eternity. Twelve eternities make for a miserable Christmas Day.

Telesa invites me to her place for Christmas dinner. I'm tired after my late night yesterday, but I accept the invitation because if I go home, I'll spend the night binging on ice cream and cereal while watching Hallmark movies. While that is my normal choice of activity after a long day at work, tonight it feels especially pathetic.

Telesa, her husband, and two kids do a good job of distracting me from my silent phone, but eventually, I have to go home.

When I pull into my parking spot, lights shine out of my windows because I was smart enough to leave them on when I left this morning. Despite the light, the place is still empty. It'll be a few days before my roommates come home. I miss them. I want someone to talk to, but Layla's still ignoring my texts, and Livy's dealing with her own drama.

I step out of my car, and ice crunches under my shoes. The snow from yesterday partially melted during the day and has now refrozen. The parking lot is slick, but if I make it to the salted sidewalk, I'll be fine. I take tiny steps and keep my balance. Until I get to a patch of invisible, smooth ice.

I slip, stumble, slip. My arms windmill to keep me upright, but it's a losing battle. If only I were wearing ice skates, I might have a chance. As it is, I'm going down.

Until someone grabs the back of my coat and holds me upright until I find my balance again.

"Are you okay?" the husky, deep voice behind me asks.

Noah. He's here.

I turn too quickly, and propel myself into his broad chest. We both tumble over, me on top of him, and land with a thud. My elbow gets him in the ribs.

"Ouch," I moan.

He groans. "That's another bruise from the ice. I'm starting to take it personally."

I roll off of him, and we both stand and make our way to the salted sidewalk where ice cannot trick us. We stare at each other, not touching. A worry line creases his forehead. Why is he here? After a long, silent day, I think the worst.

"Come upstairs?" I ask.

He nods. "Yeah, that would be good."

He follows me into the building and up to my apartment on the third floor. Neither of us speaks. I'm waiting for him to break the silence, but he must be waiting for the same thing from me.

It takes a minute to get my key in the lock, but once we're inside, I drop my purse on a kitchen chair and say, "I thought you were staying at Nordquest through Saturday. Why are you here now?"

He grimaces. "Do you not want me here? Do you want me to leave?"

"No," I say quickly. "I want to know why you haven't called or texted like you promised."

He jerks back as if I slapped him. "I called. And texted. You never answered. I was worried you decided the doctor you work with is a better boyfriend than I am."

I'm taken off guard. "What does Doug have to do with anything?"

"Your dad said you were out with friends last night, and I can only assume you were with him at the bar. Then you never responded to any of my messages."

"I promise, I never got any message from you."

"Is my number still blocked?"

I yank my phone from my pocket, afraid I didn't unblock his number like I thought. No, it's unblocked.

I show him the empty chat screen. "I have nothing from you. What number did you call?"

He rattles off a number.

"You memorized it?" I ask.

"In high school. Which is good, because my phone shattered soon after we ... ah, you know, stopped talking, and I hadn't backed up my contacts."

I laugh. Relief spreading through me. "Well, you memorized it wrong. The last number is a seven, not one."

His jaw drops. "What! No."

"Yep." I wait a beat. "I wonder who you've been texting."

He grimaces. "That has the potential to be very embarrassing."

"You called me," I say, this time in a whisper.

"I tried to call you." He takes a step closer. "When you didn't answer all day, Matt drove me down the mountain."

My nose wrinkles at the mention of my brother. "Why would he do that? Is he still here?"

"No, he left as soon as we saw you pull up. He drove me down because he watched me panic all day and couldn't take another minute of my pining. He also feels bad about how he kept us apart for so long."

"As he should."

"He wanted me to tell you as soon as you're ready to talk to him, he'd like to make it up to you."

Having Noah here with me, knowing Matt isn't forcing him to choose between us, helps. Maybe someday I'll let him apologize in person. Not really what I want to think about right now.

Noah opens his arms and I fall into his embrace. This is what I've been craving since yesterday. He is the best Christmas gift.

"I have an idea for a Christmas movie," he says into my hair.

I chuckle. "You went from hating Hallmark to wanting to write for them?"

He leads me to the couch, and we sit. His arm goes over my shoulders, and I lean into his side. Wherever we are, in his arms is my favorite spot to be.

"Do you want to hear about my movie plot?" he asks.

I mostly want him to kiss me, but I can be patient. "Sure."

"Our main characters, Jonah and Gem, were—"

I burst out laughing and lay my head back to look at him. "Jonah? Why isn't he called Noah?"

He shakes his head and suppresses a smile. "This is a movie. This isn't about us."

"Oh, right. My mistake. So, the only similarity is that Jonah and Noah had adventures on the high seas?"

"Essentially." He pulls me close again. "Jonah and Gem were best friends in high school. Gem was the only good thing Jonah had in his life for a long time, but he screwed up and let her get away. Years passed, but he never got over her. Girlfriends came and went—"

I growl at the mention of girlfriends. "Just how many did he have over these years?"

"Not important. They went their way, and he went his. Separate ways. None of them could claim the part of his heart he'd given to Gem when they were teens."

"Noah," I whisper. It's so sweet and completely relatable, because I've felt the same way over the years.

I place my palm on his solid, warm chest. I can feel his heartbeat. I snuggle in closer.

He kisses the top of my head. "Then Jonah's lucky day came. Five days before Christmas, he saves her life. She isn't filled with gratitude at his fast reflexes like any other woman would have been in the same circumstances."

"Ha!"

"She's still brokenhearted and tormented by how he treated her all those years ago. She'd never been able to move on—"

"That's a little dramatic, don't you think?"

"Do you want to hear this story or not?"

"I guess so," I grumble. "But only if you don't make me sound pathetic."

"This is about Jonah and Gem. Nothing to do with us."

"Sorry, I forgot. Please continue."

He laughs. "As luck would have it, they're stuck together at a ski resort. There's no escape for Gem, and Jonah sees his chance. He uses his most powerful wooing techniques on her."

I snort. "Those were your most powerful wooing techniques?"

"They worked didn't they?" He kisses my temple, and I don't argue further. "Through his skill, she softens and forgives him for being an idiot in high school. Unfortunately for Noah, Gem had another guy interested. A doctor. She went off to have drinks with this doctor and Noah panicked—"

"You mean Jonah."

"Right. *Jonah* panicked. He chased after Gem and professed his undying adoration for her."

"Is that what you're doing? Professing your undying adoration?"

He continues as if I didn't interrupt.

"'Gem! Gem!' Jonah called from outside her apartment

window. With a boombox, because that's romantic. 'I like you a lot, and I think we have a chance at love. Please choose me, and not the perfect doctor. I may not be perfect, but I will buy you twenty books every December.'"

I stifle a giggle and hide my smile in his chest. "He's yelling so the entire neighborhood can witness his book vow?"

"Yes, because that's also romantic."

"What happens next?" I ask.

I feel his shrug against my cheek.

"I'm not sure how it ends," he says. "I thought maybe you could help me. What does Gem decide to do?"

I run my finger along his abs as I think. "After telling Jonah to be quiet and not wake her neighbors, she invites him inside, tells him there is nothing going on with the handsome, suave, rich, perfect doctor, and gives him a mug of hot air. 'I choose you,' she says."

He sighs, as if letting go of all his worry in one great breath. "I hoped that was how this would end."

He leans away, and from his pocket, he pulls out an origami star and hands it to me.

"What is this?" I ask.

"My Christmas wish."

I unfold the star slowly. Written across the center is *I wish for Meg to forgive me and to let me be her friend again. I miss her.*

Then he holds out the other origami star.

"Is that my wish?" I ask.

"Yep. Shall I read it?"

I take it from his hand and tear it into teeny tiny pieces and toss them into the air like confetti.

"No," I say. "Let's just say I'm glad your wish came true and not mine."

He laughs. "Okay."

"Out of all the Christmas movies I've ever seen, and that is a lot, I like our movie the best of them all. Except it needs one thing."

"What's that?"

"The heroine needs her Christmas movie kiss, Jonah."

The smile that stretches across his face is perfect. "Anytime, Gem."

He kisses me in a way that would have millions of viewers swoon, but too bad for them, it's meant for only us.

Epilogue

SEPTEMBER

MEG

The sun is warm on my skin. I should lather on another layer of sunscreen, or I will roast, but I can't find the energy to move.

Noah, me, Matt, and Matt's girlfriend Tabby are spending a day at the beach before we board our Bahama cruise. The four of us flew out to Florida a few days early. Mom and Dad will arrive tonight. Tomorrow we board the ship.

This is the first time since December that Matt and I have spent significant time together. Over the last eight months, he's called a few times and we text occasionally. When I visit Mom and Dad every month, he stops by for dinner at least one night while I'm there. I no longer seek after his time, but he's now willing to share it without complaint.

I was nervous about this vacation before we left, but it hasn't been awkward like I expected. Tabby has helped a lot. Not only is she friendly and fun, but she also makes us two pairs, with no spare.

Matt met her at a New Year's party last year. I didn't think their relationship would last, because Matt's girlfriends never do, but they're still going strong. He might actually love her. I hope they never break up because I like her.

"I'm ready for another dip in the water," Tabby says. Her lounge chair groans as she sits up. "Anyone else?"

"Me," Matt says.

"I'm not finished baking yet," I say.

"I'll stay with Meg," Noah says.

He reaches over and takes my hand, entwining our fingers. My smile grows. I love him more than I knew was possible.

I'm looking forward to another week of vacationing together, especially with my parents. I need to soak up as much time with my family because starting in January, I'll be a traveling nurse. My first post is six months in New Orleans. A lot of what Noah does can be done remotely, and he'll make his home base wherever I am. Neither of us will have to travel alone any longer.

"Oh, crap," Noah says.

He lets go of my hand, and I immediately miss his touch.

I crack an eye. "What?"

He rolls off the beach lounger, gets down on the ground, and starts rummaging around in the sand.

"I dropped something," he says.

I sit up and swing my feet over the side. "What did you lose?"

"Oh, here it is."

He straightens so he's still on his knees but facing me, and in his hand is an open ring box. Nestled in the velvet is a diamond ring surrounded by red and green rhinestones. My breath hitches. It's a beautiful ring, though it quickly blurs as tears spring to my eyes.

"It looks like Christmas," I breathe out.

"It is your favorite."

"You are my favorite."

It's such a cheesy line, but Noah doesn't crack a smile. He's too busy studying me.

"Does that mean you'll marry me?" he asks, the fervor in his voice touching me almost like a caress.

I swallow down all the emotion rising up in my chest. "Is this you asking?"

He ducks his head as he laughs softly. "Meg Wright, I love you. You're the family I've dreamed about my whole life. Every day with you is like living in a fantasy. Will you marry me?"

I can't hold back. I throw myself into his arms. "Yes!"

And then, like all great love stories, the hero and heroine make out on the beach as the ending credits roll.

I hoped you enjoyed *Her Christmas Movie Kiss!* If so, please let other readers know. A great way to support authors is by leaving a review on Amazon, Goodreads, or BookBub. A star rating is enough to make a difference!

If you'd like to be notified about future releases, sign up for my newsletter through my website, gracejcroy.com, or by following the QR code. When you sign up, you'll receive my novella, *Kiss Me, Jane,* for free.

Also by Grace J. Croy

It Must Be Love Series

It's Not Like It's a Secret

It's Not Like It's Fate

It's Not Like It's Real

Christmas Wishes Series

Her Christmas Rescue

Her Christmas Movie Kiss

Her Counterfeit Christmas

Magical Regency Series

Intuition

Bronwyn

Stand-Alone Titles

The Lonely Lips Club

Love Checks In

About the Author

Grace's favorite things include reading, writing, traveling, and her cats.

She lives in Utah, in a little house at the bottom of a little mountain, where the snow piles high in the winter.

When she isn't writing, she works as a librarian, planning awesome community events and advising readers on what book to try next.

Her favorite places to travel include New Zealand, California, and Paris. No matter how long she's away, she always loves coming home.

Made in the USA
Columbia, SC
14 August 2024

40042144R00140